D1474828

Hut of Fallen Persimmons

Hut of Fallen Persimmons

Adriana Lisboa

Translated from the Portuguese by Sarah Green

Texas Tech University Press

This book is typeset in Monotype Fairfield. The paper used in this book meets the
minimum requirements of ANSI/NISO Z39.48-1992 (R1997). ∞

Library of Congress Cataloging-in-Publication Data
Lisboa, Adriana, 1970–
    [Rakushisha. English]
        Hut of fallen persimmons / Adriana Lisboa ; translated from the Portuguese
    by Sarah Green.
            p. cm. — (The Americas series)
    Summary: "A journey to Japan seen through the eyes of two Brazilians: Haruki
    and Celina. Through a counterpoint of narration and text, and with reference to
    haiku by seventeenth-century master Matsuo Basho, the pair's losses and
    struggles unfold"—Provided by publisher.
    Includes haiku by Matsuo Basho in English and Japanese.
    ISBN 978-0-89672-721-2 (hardcover : alk. paper)
    1. Brazilians—Japan—Fiction. 2. Brazilians—Travel—Japan—Fiction. 3. Man-
    woman relationships—Fiction. 4. Japan—Description and travel—Fiction. 5.
    Haiku—Translations into English. I. Green, Sarah, 1946- II. Matsuo, Basho,
    1644–1694. III. Title.
        PQ9698.422.I73R3513 2011
        869.3'42—dc22   2011000695

Obra publicada com o apoio do Ministério da Cultura do Brasil / Fundação Biblioteca
Nacional / Coordenadoria Geral do Livro e da Leitura

Work published with the aid of the Brazilian Ministry of Culture / National Library
Foundation / General Department of Books and Reading

Texas Tech University Press | Box 41037 | Lubbock, Texas 79409-1037 USA
800.832.4042 | ttup@ttu.edu | www.ttupress.org

To Gabriel

Amar é um elo
entre o azul
e o amarelo

Love is a link
between blue
and yellow

PAULO LEMINSKI

Hut of Fallen Persimmons

JUNE 17TH

In order to walk, you just have to put one foot in front of the other. One foot in front of the other. It's not complicated. It's not difficult. You can keep small goals in mind: first just to the intersection. That crosswalk at the traffic light and that man with a transparent umbrella and a dog in a yellow raincoat, waiting to cross.

The dog appears to be a Labrador and looks at me as I approach.

It has a friendly face. We're both Westerners, my friend. Although perhaps you were born here, right? Were you? At some breeder's kennel? Of course, where else, you answer me, with the patience of Labradors.

I wasn't born here. I don't know if you're particularly interested in knowing that. I'm from the other side of the planet. You might say I came hidden in another person's luggage. It's as if I had entered illegally, in spite of the visa in my passport. On tiptoes, so that no one could see me, so that no one could see the invisible things I brought in my suitcase. I hope that even now no one can see me, that no one suspects. In that sense, I'm much more of a Westerner than you, my yellow-raincoated friend. I don't belong in this place.

And so why, exactly, am I here, you might ask me if we had more time to exchange glances, if your collar and your owner weren't already pulling you toward your obligations—whatever they might be, companion, guide, playmate.

I don't really know, to be honest. I was learning to walk again. I am learning to walk again. After the storm, the ice age, the great drought, we can use whatever image we please, no one is going to care very much, after all who are we if not less than anonymous here. This door just opened. I don't have time right now to tell you how it all happened. And I still don't know if walking is the same as remembering, the same as forgetting, and which of the two is my remedy, if neither of them, if there are no options and if walking is the disease and the remedy, the poison that weaves death and the drug that can cure. If I have come to remember—if I have come to forget. If I have come to die or to be immunized. Perhaps I'll discover. Perhaps it'll never be possible to discover, to unveil, to raise the awning, to remove any trace of an illusion of the illusion of walking.

Whatever the case may be. It's just a matter of putting one foot in front of the other.

One foot in front of the other. Ignore the weight of my legs. After all, this body of mine is a machine that has no reason to have defects, not yet, this body has seen only a bit more than three decades, it's possible that it's programmed for many more. Is it? I don't know, I don't care to know, but it's possible that it is. One would assume that all my muscles are in their proper place, and the bones beneath them, and the synapses transmitting the intentions—no, not the intentions, the determinations, the orders of the brain. That tyrant. Do that, he says. Move. And the legs move. That's it. It must be like that, very simple. Just move like a Labrador in a yellow raincoat led by its owner along the crosswalk.

I can go very slowly, at my own rate of slowness, because I'm alone. I can choose the rhythm of my difficulty in walking, the rhythm of the weight of my legs.

My umbrella hides a piece of the sky and the rain falls softly, but I insisted on coming out in sandals and my feet are getting wet. What to do. That's not the most important thing, not by a long shot. Whether they're wet or whether they're dry. I can feel the dampness slightly cold on my skin. The important thing is that they continue to take turns on the sidewalk, if ever so slowly.

I have found my pace. The Labrador and its owner are up ahead. It's strange, the feeling that I will never see them again, and yet, it's much more likely that I will run into creatures that I will never see again rather than the contrary. I wonder if life is perhaps made of only chance encounters. Perhaps made even more so of tangents, of peripheral movements, of fleeting glances that dissipate in the next instance. Why stay put, then? Why not simply travel? But the gravity of loss pulls on me as the man and the dog, the transparent umbrella and the yellow raincoat, draw away, with their backs to me. With the exception of those two, I am alone on the street. Even more so because of the rain. The occasional car goes by and Bus no. 20.

This is the truth to be found in traveling. I hadn't realized.

Traveling teaches us a few things. That life is a path and not a fixed point in space. That we are like the passage of the days and the months and the years, as the Japanese poet Matsuo Bashō wrote in a travel diary, and that the one thing we do indeed possess, our only asset, is our capacity of locomotion. It is our talent for traveling.

This area is fairly quiet, generally speaking. A relatively new neighborhood in Kyoto, they told me. It lies at the foot of the mountain, at the edge of a forest that will perhaps have disappeared within a few decades, making way for more houses like the ones I see, of well-heeled people, so it appears to me. They must be. Farther up are veritable mansions, the majority constructed in modern architectural styles, but one of them reminds me of a centuries-old Zen temple. I wonder if it has been here for a long time, if it is truly old, or just the property of some old-fashioned eccentric.

Or if such a thing as old-fashioned exists in Japan.

How things coexist here I don't quite understand yet, I may never understand, I've seen girls in kimonos buying Hello Kitty products, I don't think I have the correct scales for that, the slide rule properly adjusted. I don't know if I possess the necessary capacity for amazement.

I memorized the name of my bus stop, because for me, everything is, and continues to be, such a labyrinth: it is called Katsurazaka Gakkō-chō mae. I take Bus no. 20 in front of the ever spotless public garden. I go to Katsura Station and from there my path may vary, depending on the day, depending on what I want or need to do. Usually I go to Karasuma by train. From there I can walk to several places or transfer to the subway at Karasuma-Ōike.

The way back is always the same, from Katsura to Katsurazaka Gakkō-chō mae on Bus no. 6. Sometimes I take a shortcut by getting off in front of the supermarket and I buy something or other. I try to decipher the labels. It took me a long time to buy dish-washing liquid; in an attempt to explain to the clerk exactly what I wanted I had to use a series of gestures. It looked as if I were playing charades.

I warm up in anticipation of the taste of the green tea, the saké, and the bean sweets. I like to take a chance and buy a different one each time, but I almost always come out on top. Sometimes I choose by the color, sometimes by the shape. I like to pass by the shelves of Swiss chocolates or the section of fine French confections and realize that the small, delicate, milky sphere of the Japanese sweet that I have selected today is, for the moment, much more tempting.

Part of the journey: bean sweet delights. Part of the path.

I have already surrounded myself with familiar things in these three weeks, but I won't be staying here much longer, I shall soon be leaving, undoing once and for all this web of affections that are mine alone, these unshared affinities, as if I were a bubble inside of Kyoto and Kyoto possessed small, secret trophies that had been saved especially for me from the time it was founded, more than one thousand years ago.

When I met Haruki, he spoke of a poem that said, Even in Kyoto I long for Kyoto.

They're building new houses in the neighborhood. During the week I can hear the noises of the work at a distance, from my room. But around here today it is as silent as a Saturday, Doyōbi, the day of the earth, as they taught me—although, as they also pointed out, noises and all sorts of sounds permeate certain areas of Kyoto: whistles and bells at the downtown crosswalks, recorded voices on the buses, trains, and subways incessantly repeating the names of the approaching stations (in Japanese, and in English where tourist spots are concerned), salespeople at commercial establishments hawking with the traditional irasshaimase, welcome! background music even on the streets, and the unbelievable noise in places where they play pachinko, a type of Japanese pinball that isn't exactly pinball, that is also something like a slot machine.

One foot in front of the other. The Labrador and its owner

turn the corner and disappear forever. I don't know the names of those plants, except for those indecently flowering azaleas, it's June, it's spring almost summer, and perhaps today will mark the onset of the rainy season that begins in earnest at this time of year.

Even in Kyoto I long for Kyoto.

But I must have small goals. One foot in front of the other. Until the weight of my legs evaporates and walking is almost easy, almost commonplace.

Haruki

They almost didn't allow Haruki to go up to the tenth floor, where the Consulate General of Japan was located in Rio de Janeiro. You'd better hurry, said the girl at the reception desk. They shut the office at 5 o'clock sharp and don't like anyone going up when it's near closing time.

He presented his ID, grabbed the card to go through the turnstile and entered the elevator out of breath, his clothes disheveled and his hair a mess, his face gleaming with sweat.

The clerk who waited on him was wearing an impeccable navy blue suit. He greeted Haruki in Japanese and Haruki found himself obliged to say that he didn't understand. He explained his situation, the category of the visa he wanted; he handed over the proper documents. The clerk in the suit said to him in a low, precise voice, please fill out this form, but do it quickly because we're closing up for the day.

Haruki felt like a foreign object. He shouldn't have been perspiring. Or if he had to be perspiring, he could at least speak rudimentary Japanese. His facial features, his name, everything imposed that responsibility on him—a responsibility to which, however, he had never deferred.

He had the basic information. He had grown up hearing some Japanese at home. Above all when his grandparents came to visit. But that was years ago, and during all those years he had had more than enough to do. And no talent whatsoever for languages. Even the syntactical regimen of verbs in Portuguese demanded his full attention. The school lessons about subjective subordinate noun clauses and about how the expression *haja vista* is only inflected when it precedes and agrees with a noun in the plural with no preposition were about as much as he could handle.

The world was not composed of letters, but of shapes and colors. The world, in other words, was watercolorable.

At his side, on a wooden bookcase filled with flyers in Japanese, a colorful, perfect origami ball observed him. The ball was larger than a closed fist, made with several pieces of paper. Haruki felt completely awkward, as if he were the antithesis of that colorful origami ball. So tardy, so untidy, and so un-Japanese—what right did he have to go around sporting a pair of slanted eyes?

It was sprinkling when he left the consulate, with the promise that his visa would be ready in two days. Category: G. Cultural activities. He opened the umbrella that he had miraculously remembered to put in his knapsack. The traffic was showing signs of day's end, the flow from downtown growing heavier.

Flamengo Park was whitewashed and opaque, coated with a thin membrane of rain. On the sidewalk, people without umbrellas hurried along: shoulders huddled in involuntary gestures of protection, frowning, taking short, rapid steps. Some covered their heads with their briefcases. With folded newspapers. Bodies pierced by the cold wind that now blew in from the beach.

Hakuri walked to the corner of Machado de Assis Street and headed down toward the subway station. Which would also be showing signs of day's end. Nothing that he wasn't accustomed to. Haruki was a user of public transportation. It had been quite a while since he had had a car. Cars, besides costing money, cost insurance, cost garages, cost flat tires, cost one day the glass shattered by a guy who stole the radio, cost parking fees and looking for parking places, cost the headlights from a insignificant collision, cost bumpers scratched and sides scratched by someone passing by with a nail or keys, and cost the fear of lightning-fast kidnappings, especially during that disastrous period between Christmas and Carnival and the police had already politely warned us that we really did have to be careful and that you didn't have to be wealthy to be a victim of a quicknapping. He once had a 1972 Volkswagen Beetle that was a shade of red bordering on burgundy. It was a nice car. It caught on fire.

The sweat on his face had dried. It was good to feel the cold wind blowing through his shirt and in his hair. Suddenly it was good to be there, in Rio de Janeiro, at that very moment, and to be who he was, an illustrator with his knapsack on his back, for an instant it was good that it was raining and to know that within ten minutes he would arrive at Largo do Machado Station.

It was good to know that there were things like the inversions of seasons in the two hemispheres, time zones, places where the sun rose as it set somewhere else. Almost science fiction–type things. It was good to know that a real Japan did indeed exist, a place where people opened their umbrellas or bewailed the lack of an umbrella, and where they stepped on a different solid ground.

Você would be happy, old man, he thought, forgetting that he had never addressed his father by the Portuguese familiar second-person form in life. Nor old man, as far as that went. Perhaps death allowed for a different type of intimacy, a lack of ceremony that he had (had he?) tried to attain in vain for forty years. Improvisations made it easier. Suddenly his father was a friend, and suddenly Haruki had just left the Japanese Consulate with the promise of a visa for cultural activities.

That very Japan, ignored for forty years and now, without warning, like a sudden start, was opening itself up to those same improvisations. It became possible, like affectionately addressing his father as *você*. A pat-on-the-back word.

Japan leaping into his life like a hiccup all because of her. Yukiko. The translator. Today, nothing more than that: the translator. Their two names were to be ironically joined together on the cover of a book. They would place their names on paper. Lovingly, coldly, flippantly.

The gentle rain turned the world luminous in Haruki's eyes. The worn-down Machado de Assis Street asphalt glistened. The parked cars glistened. The leaves of the trees. The ironwork fences in front of the buildings. Even the sounds of things glistened in the rain, the car wheels on the asphalt, the screech of a car suddenly braking and the honk of a horn, the doorman's radio blaring.

It was necessary to recognize and revere these moments. They were fleeting and rare. Moments during which for no apparent reason everything seemed to get on track, to adapt, to fall into place. All questions and the need for them disappeared. As did rushing, having a place to go, coming from some place. Simply the soles of shoes striking the wet sidewalk and there you have it, the world needed no other meaning.

One foot in front of the other.

Fleeting, rare moments. That particular one dissipated suddenly, at the corner of Catete Street. Haruki realized that he was losing something, he even glanced back automatically, to see if a piece of himself had fallen on the sidewalk. But it was the instant that was disintegrating, a spoon of salt in water. And Haruki stirred the spoon, disintegrated the instant, because it could not be otherwise, if we do not kill our epiphanies, they will kill us, and he crossed the street in the familiar direction of the subway entrance.

On the short ride to Botafogo Station he did what he always did. He pulled a book out of his backpack—it would frequently be related to whatever he was at the moment illustrating or preparing to illustrate.

That afternoon, standing up, somewhat squeezed in by the other passengers, he pulled out the book that had started everything.

True, there was a certain pleasure in that: to take out a book in Japanese and leaf through it with interest, as if he could actually understand something. As if the reasons that had caused him to check it out of the library, that very afternoon, were not merely aesthetic, only to see that pile of indecipherable graphic signs together and try to see if they could contribute to his illustrations. To turn the pages to one side, then to the other, and out of the corner of his eye watch the reactions of those nearest to him, the indiscreet stares.

In the subway car, immense scarlet fingernails here. A gold wedding band. Short, chewed-down fingernails there. Conversations. End-of-workday faces. The odor of sweat. As well as of sweet perfume. There was a quick stop at Flamengo Station. Haruki finally got off at Botafogo Station and heard a voice at his side, the voice of a woman, as if it were tugging at his sleeve, a voice so different from the surrounding background voices that were fading there on the subway platform: Excuse me, but I was just so curious. Was that book you were reading in Japanese or Chinese?

Half an hour later, they were having a cup of coffee and exchanging looks of curiosity and indecisiveness over their table.

The woman now had a name: Celina. And, in keeping with that name, it appeared to Haruki that she was actually something volatile. As if perhaps on the inside she had neither bones nor muscles nor viscera but rather air. A piece of sky covered by a thin human epidermis. A piece of sky almost human. On the outside, hers was the saddest smile that he had seen in recent times.

For half an hour Haruki alone spoke almost the entire time, giving an erratic summary of his completely un-Japanese life that was now cross-dressing with a book in Japanese.

First, still at the subway, he had explained to Celina: It's Japanese, but I wasn't reading the book, I was just leafing through it. I don't speak Japanese. Do you see those symbols? They could be Greek. They could be Russian. I don't know any of them. I don't have the slightest idea what they could possibly mean.

You looked like you were reading, she said.

He shrugged.

I have a job I need to do on this book. I was just looking at it.

Silence on her part for a few seconds. But afterward her insistent curiosity. You have to do a job on a book you can't read?

They were on their way up the subway escalator. Haruki realized that she would not be satisfied with evasive answers. It seemed she wanted to know what a guy with Japanese features was doing with his nose stuck in a book in Japanese if he didn't understand one word. Put that way, it was quite a significant mystery—due above all to its apparent triviality.

And then would his masculinity determine that he take a woman who had approached him at the subway exit for a cup of coffee (and, who knows, to his house and to his bed)? He thought about that for a moment. Almost pragmatically.

He wanted to talk about the book. He had not yet had a serious conversation with anyone about the job.

It was a job that was also scary, for several reasons. It cast shadows. It made dark noises. It rubbed against his skin with long paws, with the drool of beasts, with the horns of devils, with allusions to another world.

Perhaps that Celina composed of sky and a sad smile had appeared precisely for that reason: to listen.

An illustration job. A trip. A visa in his passport—a passport that had cost him an afternoon-long pilgrimage to the Federal Police, before taking it to the Japanese Consulate.

I illustrate books, he said. Usually children's books. This time they asked me to do something different.

He stopped, in the midst of the human flow, on the subway platform and showed the book to Celina. A rash move.

This is a diary by Bashō. A Japanese poet. Seventeenth century, he said. It's the first time this diary is being translated here in Brazil, they asked me to illustrate the translation. They already sent it to me, I've read it, but I wanted to get the original from the library. I just wanted to know what the text was like, visually.

Celina was walking with her head down.

I think that I would do the same thing, she said. Even if I didn't understand a word, like you. Just to see it, just to have the original text in my hands.

He turned toward her as they passed through the turnstiles, at the exit.

Would you like to go have a cup of coffee?

And now they had been getting to know each other for half an hour, half an hour and a few minutes, over a table and two empty coffee cups.

They already had a history of settings: the subway, the sidewalk, and the now rainless street, the bookstore where they had entered to have a cup of coffee. At that point they knew, among other things, the following about one another: that Celina drank her coffee black, that Haruki drank his with two level spoonfuls of sugar.

At the core of their curiosity and indecisiveness, a quasi-intimacy.

Celina

Forget about tomorrow is another day. And forget about time goes by—no more of that from here on. There were no types of projections beyond the exact instant of that particular heartbeat. The future no longer existed. The past did indeed exist, even if it was murky and fluid. But not the future.

She had had to learn how to walk again. One day Celina realized that the most important part of her body was her feet. Wherever her feet were at the moment, there would be her soul, or whatever it's called, she thought, that part of her body that always threatened to outdo her own body.

Her soul trod the ground and lived in the space occupied by two anatomical complexes, a pair of ankles, heels, tarsi, metatarsi, and ten toes. Her soul jostled with two times twenty-six bones.

When she finally came to, after a year or something to that effect, her feet, with her soul on board, had put her into that situation, which she knew to be entirely in the present, and only that: She lived in a one-bedroom apartment on the top floor of a tiny building, in the Grajaú neighborhood. She owned a large worktable and a sewing machine.

She made cloth purses to sell. They were beautiful. She sold them, and that's how she made a living.

She embroidered the purses and as she sewed she counted the stitches, she let herself become hypnotized by the numbers. She gave testimony to her present, thirty-six years of her heart beating between sixty and one hundred beats per minute—totaling more than one billion heartbeats—and she was lucky that her muscle could handle numbers of such grandeur.

She thought back to her grandmother, who had been an embroiderer. It was easy to think about her, her grandmother who had been born in Nazaré da Mata, who had raised twenty-three children. Of those, only five had been born of her womb. The others were the children of her husband's six other women. And she thought of her mother, a dressmaker for socialites, who had created patterns and embroidered in Recife.

Celina made a purse in honor of each one of her aunts and uncles.

She embroidered a purse in honor of the Afro-Brazilian *Umbanda* magic that, they said, had finally made her mother become pregnant.

She also managed to recreate, with her needle and thread, the house where she had been born, and which had been swept away by the great flood in the June of her birth.

She had been thinking about her grandmother, about her mother, and about the flood when she saw embroidery-like figures on the cover of a book that a man was reading in the subway car. Could they be Japanese or Chinese?

A man with Asian features was reading the book, standing up, on the subway. Celina lowered her eyes to her own feet. It was sprinkling outside, and she hadn't brought her umbrella. She had reached the subway by ducking under the marquees, getting slightly wet. She then looked back at the man who was reading so intently. And then the almost irresistible curiosity to know what it was, who had written it, what it was about. What sort of flood, genealogy, what *Orixá* or *Umbanda* god might those black and white embroideries on paper represent?

If I could manage to ask him, Celina thought—or even better, Celina made a deal with herself, if I could manage to get close to him and ask the question it will immediately stop raining.

She waited until they passed Flamengo Station. She watched to see if he would get off, he didn't. There wasn't much time before the end of the line, but the car was so full she would first have to get closer to him, and how to do it, and how to pose the question—say excuse me, clear her throat?

At Botafogo Station, which by coincidence was where she also needed to get off (And what to do if he continued on? Continue on as well? And what would happen to the magic about the rain? And if she were unable to get close to him and ask the question— would it then rain forever?), the man with Asian features closed the book and turned toward the car door. He was thrown slightly off his feet as the train braked. He instinctively recovered his balance by leaning his body in the opposite direction.

Celina straightened up and moved forward. As they got off, she caught up to him while they were still on the platform: Excuse me, but I was just so curious. Was that book you were reading in Japanese or Chinese?

JUNE 18TH (*Morning*)

We were both dressed as clowns, Marco and I, in my dream. The same outfits, green and white. We each carried a green parasol. The clothes, the makeup, the parasols, everything united and equated us and perhaps for that reason we negated each other. It was almost as if we were the same person. There were periods, or moments, at least, in which we were indeed the same person. For better or for worse. There were times it would be impossible to say what belonged to one, what belonged to the other. I stopped cracking my knuckles because Marco hated that. He learned to pronounce the word gearshift correctly because I would always complain about the way he said it. And all of a sudden, the magic: I was unable to crack my knuckles, even if Marco was nowhere around.

In my dream, however, we weren't magicians, but rather clowns, and victims of an absolutely ridiculous robbery. Worthy of a pair of clowns. The robber was a small elderly Japanese man on foot. Marco and I were on a bicycle, only one bicycle, he seated on the back and I struggling to pedal due to the weight. I pedaled and pedaled, trying to move forward and escape from the little old robber, but the old man was running right next to us and was reaching out to grab whatever I might be carrying in my green-and-white clown purse.

At that point the parasols had disappeared and the scenery, which had previously been urban, began to give way to a dirt road with very beautiful, sunlit fields on either side. Possibly rice fields like those I have seen recently. An occasional person on foot walked down the road.

The Japanese robber finally fell behind. He was another chapter in the dream. I now rode the bicycle with confidence, and began to pick up speed.

But Marco fell asleep. He toppled off the bicycle, and not even the fall awakened him. He remained lying in the middle of the road. When I realized that he had fallen off and I looked back, Marco slept on, a rolled-up body, a body somehow piled on top of itself, a motionless shape on the dirt. Totally alien, Marco was suddenly no longer my green-and-white twin clown, but rather the most remote spot on earth. Marco was unattainable, forever separate, strange, foreign.

It is still dark when I awake, the vestige of my dream is almost a physical sensation. The sunlight will soon invade my room, it's June, almost summer in the Northern Hemisphere, and day breaks very early. The shutters on the windows and the door to the veranda do little to soften the brightness. This bothers me a little. The light and my sleepiness, my sleepiness and the light. They fight one another.

I've never thought about having a diary. Not even as a young girl, not even as an adolescent. Conceivably I am only doing this now because I couldn't resist the paper they make here in Japan. There's a shop quite close to the Kyoto National Museum. There are countless shops that specialize in paper, true, but this particular one appealed to me. Yesterday I made a rather frustrating visit to the museum, some of the rooms were closed. As I left, I came across this store.

I don't know how long I stayed in there, in my almost incommunicado Western bubble, but I had the feeling that I spent more time there than at the museum.

Every shelf was its own particular universe of colors, of textures.

There were large rolls of handcrafted paper sold by the meter. There were minuscule packages with cards. There were things that I had no idea what they were used for but that fascinated me nonetheless.

I bought this notebook. The notebook became a diary. It was only later that I remembered about Matsuo Bashō and his *Saga nikki,* the diary that Bashō wrote near here, when he visited his disciple Mukai Kyorai for the second time.

Legend has it that Kyorai had close to forty persimmon trees growing in the garden of his house in Saga, then a suburb of Kyoto. He had agreed to sell the persimmons one autumn when the trees were heavily laden with fruit, but the evening before he was to deliver them, a violent storm hit. There was not a single persimmon left. From that day forward Kyorai referred to his house as Rakushisha, the Hut of Fallen Persimmons.

Haruki and Celina

One of the films shown on the plane was *The Godfather*.
Haruki started watching, it was the fourth or fifth time he had
seen that film. But he was once again shocked when the movie
producer woke up to that eloquent message from Don Vito Cor-
leone, the horse's decapitated head in his bed.

The headsets did not mask the roar of the airplane's engines;
their seats were right over the wings. On his tray there still rested
a half-empty glass of orange juice. With two gulps Haruki downed
the awful processed juice, made slightly less awful with two or
three ice cubes.

He tore his eyes away from the film, the voices droned on
through the earphones, overlapping the sound of the engines. He
knew that outside there were lights on the tips of the wings and
the compact darkness of the night and the inhuman temperatures
and the lack of oxygen. It would take nothing more than a mere
pop to die.

He closed his eyes. He removed the headset.

Next to him, Celina was asleep. It gave him the opportunity to
discover that Celina had a weightless manner of sleeping. It was
the first time he had seen her like that. She seemed to no longer

exist, to migrate into some other dimension, and what remained behind was nothing more than a ghost, a hologram saving her place. For her to claim when she needed it. Perhaps she didn't even breathe while asleep.

They were flying over the Atlantic, ten days after having met on the subway and having sat down for a cup of coffee.

Haruki had talked and talked and talked, during that cup of coffee, about his new job, about the illustrations for the poet Bashō's diary, written more than three hundred years earlier.

And now I'm going to Japan, he said that afternoon. A research trip, at the end of May. I received a grant, they paid for the airplane ticket as well.

Celina glanced at her watch. Five more minutes and she would miss her doctor's appointment. She said so to Haruki.

Is he near here, your doctor?

A block away.

So you can make it on time.

Yes, I can.

A moment of silence, Celina checked her watch again.

And you, she asked.

I live close by.

Hmm, I live in Grajaú.

Another moment of silence, and everything was breaking down into alternatives.

You know what? We could get together for a bite to eat when you leave the doctor's office, Haruki said.

Yes, that would be great.

And so things began to happen between the two of them, almost as if by chance, but seemingly definitive. With a Never Again raising its head the whole time, it would have sufficed to say it was nice to have met you, it would have sufficed not to exchange telephone numbers nor e-mails and bury chance under the lime of wisdom—nothing could be definitive, and encounters might last two hours or two decades or two times that, but at some point in time it would by necessity be the end. Of all the great love affairs. Of all the small ones. Of all the oaths, the promises, all the for-better-or-worses. Of all the non-affairs, the disaffections, estrangements, the marriages forever after, the resentments forever after, of all the parallels that were possible only in the abstraction of geometry, of all the small passions and all the great passions, of everything that dies in the entrance hall of passion, of all the unlived ties, of everything.

They had dinner and drank quite a bit. They split the bill. On leaving, Haruki went with her to catch a cab, both of them weaving a little.

Neither one spoke of staying together for the evening: neither nearby, where Haruki lived and illustrated books, nor in Grajaú, where Celina made cloth purses.

It didn't have to last. No need for promises. It could be just one night of slightly drunken sex, and that would be it. If one way or another, at some point in time, it was doomed to end. But no one touched on the subject.

On the contrary, he held open the door of the taxi for Celina to get in and startled her for the last time that evening, although it would not be the last time for them to experience that sensation.

Listen, he said.

She looked up at Haruki from inside the cab, that woman composed of air, of sky, of a sad smile. Her eyes were luminous, under the effect of the alcohol.

You could go to Japan with me.

Sex. It had been a while. For six years, sex had become a haphazard affair. One or another fortuitous tryst might happen. Gratuitously. If Celina's feet happened to be pointed in that direction.

Encounters attached to the narrow frame of impossibility. And the pleasure, that pleasure was hard, a chunk of stone. Arid. Bitter. Sad.

Celina didn't want anyone in her life. It wasn't anything like a decision that had been formulated after a great deal of consideration and then put into practice. It was more like verification. Like looking out the window and checking on the weather: sunny, overcast, a threat of rain.

The embroidery work on her purses was always more or less irregular. Like the purses themselves, no two were ever alike. It was deliberate that Celina always bought small quantities of any particular fabric. The purses were made when they were made. Instantly: at that instant. She had no plans for them nor for anything else, there couldn't be any, Celina wasn't going to fall for that scam.

That's a little how it was with sex. The difference being that sewing was an integral part of her life, whereas the sex was sporadic.

It had been a while, when she met Haruki. The first thing she thought of when he made that invitation, at the door of her cab, as he stood on São Clemente's sidewalk, was sex.

And for that reason she had wanted to answer no. No to committing to sex, to sharing the same bed, to performing caresses, no to the sudden idea of going to Japan possibly (probably) as Haruki's official lover and having to share her body with him every day.

Celina knew what that could mean. She needed to stay alert as to her own movements, to the ground beneath her feet. She couldn't allow herself the luxury of the inattentiveness that sex demanded. She had to stay alert.

One thing leads to another and it is all about taking immense risks, as well she knew. As she had learned six years earlier: no, it was not about simply being disappointed in love, like scraping the knees within the heart; things heal, they form scabs, sometimes you pick the scab off and the wound bleeds again, but the new skin eventually covers the old heartache. No, it was not about a simple streak of bad luck, tripping, being frustrated.

It was greater, more serious, much darker than the warning she had once received.

You could go with me to Japan, Haruki said.

Who knows, she answered.

Haruki did not close the door to the cab. He stood there, on the São Clemente sidewalk, and suddenly he looked very handsome to Celina—at the moment he turned his head slightly to the side, his eyes appearing to search out something that was already there. Scandalously visible, like all truly important things.

After a few seconds he smiled, closed the taxi door, and looking back, Celina saw that he turned away and began to walk home.

Books must await him. Colors, paints, papers. Projects. Deadlines.

Who knows, she answered.

JUNE 18TH (*Afternoon*)

The key word: trust. The first time I took the bus it was Bus no. 20. I was supposed to get off at Katsura Station, where I would continue by train to Karasuma Station, in the city center, almost to the banks of the Kamo River. I asked for information: How do I pay the bus fare? Directly to the white-gloved driver? Was there a ticket seller? No—said the Australian that I met at the bus stop. You just have to pull the ticket out of the machine when you enter the bus through the back door. When you get off the bus, by the front door, you deposit the ticket and the correct fare, based on the distance you rode. In your case, 230 yen. And who checks it, I asked the Australian. I don't know, I don't think anyone does, he said.

Although she was slightly inebriated, Celina arrived home, at her apartment in Grajaú, and went to look for a piece of fabric she had been saving for quite some time. It was a flowered print in red hues, which had suddenly come to mind as being somehow evocative of Japan.

She browsed through her books. She found a photograph and a description of traditional Japanese clothing. She pored over the women's attire.

The printed kimono was fastened with the obi, the wide sash between the waist and the breasts, which was of a different pattern. It was exactly what Celina wanted. Two designs. She searched for another piece of material, with a white background, which she also knew she had, somewhere in her closet. It was there.

A purse for Japan. For the invitation that Haruki had made less than an hour earlier. The invitation to which she had responded: Who knows. And who, indeed, would know.

The purse would be offered for sale, like all her other purses. But there, at that moment, the fabric slid between Celina's fingers and through the blades of her scissors. She chose the pattern and measured. She started to cut, and as she cut she felt her eyes burning, and all of that was good.

She cut out the fabric with dry eyes, she reproduced that cut that she had by necessity made one day, one certain day, and as she sewed, she resewed the bones of her feet very tightly to one another and sewed her detached soul on with buttons to keep it very close to the soles of her feet, and as she embroidered, she counted her stitches, one, two, ten, thirty, the embroidery masking her thoughts.

And all of that was good.

Until she felt tired. The quiet, tired night.

It was good to work. Working put things back on the right track.

Celina left her sewing on the top of the table. She rested her elbows on the worn-down wood. She regarded her arms. She stroked her right arm with her left hand, from the wrist up to the shoulder. She found her T-shirt. She found her right breast.

Quiet and tired, she remembered Marco. In front of the fishermen's colony at the Lagoa, the lagoon in Rio, where they had agreed to meet, so long ago. Marco arrived late, sweaty and smiling, with a bottle of mineral water in his hand. Celina was lying down on a bench. So many years ago. The milder heat of April. How many years ago—thirteen? Before Grajaú, before the cloth purses. Long before, very long before Haruki and the invitation to go to Japan that for some reason she tended to take seriously.

Celina had been twenty-three at the time. She was about to graduate. Full of books and ideas. Marco, running late, sweaty and smiling, hugged her so effortlessly, hugged her and the dress that she was wearing and that she resisted throwing away for so many years, even when it became worn out. From there they went to hide between four walls.

Sex was something else. Celina could take all the risks. She could close her eyes. She could waver and not know where she was, if on the ground, if in the clouds. She could feel, like someone who dives into the icy waves of the ocean, Marco's hands on her body, the first time. On her breasts. On her hips and lower still, and on the curve of her thighs. That's what sex was. It allowed for any amount of density, for any amount of subatomic particle pressure, for any interchanges with parallel universes. It involved no risks.

On that particular afternoon, they hadn't had lunch yet. They shared a dish of pasta at the motel, laughing, seated at the table, and they were as promising as young, beautiful television stars.

While he showered, she lay in bed humming "Peter Gast": I can fly and my muscles are tensed.

Then he said: You were singing to me.

And she: No I was not.

And he: Yes you were, look at you, lying on your stomach in bed facing the bathroom door.

And outside the whole world was composed of icy ocean waves.

JUNE 19TH

On the first afternoon that it rained after I arrived, the bicycles made me nervous. So many people on bicycles. And the countless women oftentimes pedaling along in high heels made me nervous. But everything settled down into a harmonic confluence that excluded only myself. It was only I who could not understand what was happening yesterday in Kyoto in the rain, while I was waiting to cross Shijō Street at rush hour.

Cars, people and bicycles, umbrellas and high heels all got along with one another. Out of place, only myself. At the root of my lack of comprehension. Biting my lips and my chewing gum between my teeth. None of the women fell, hands conducted bicycles and umbrellas like talented maestros, cars stopped at pedestrian crossings, and the padded silence of rain falling at the worst time of day—when apparently everyone got off work—frightened me like an undue dream.

Those people on bicycles demonstrated a skill comparable to Alice's. I had not yet spoken to Haruki about Alice, in the days that we were together in Kyoto, before he left for Tokyo at 185 miles per hour.

There is a Bashō Museum in Tokyo. Where Bashō lived, on the banks of the Sumida River, according to what Haruki told me.

The poet's pseudonym—the name that has followed him up to the present, to Haruki, and through Haruki to me—means banana.

Bashō, the plant, is a decorative species. A banana tree without edible fruit. It was customarily planted in the gardens of the temples. It swayed in the breeze and was ripped apart in the strong autumn winds, its long leaves were bent down by torrential rains, like the ears of a sad dog, and they glistened under the sun, when there was sun, green with solid determination.

For the banana tree poet, the tree with no edible bananas was a charming and free-spirited symbol of uselessness: his sister.

Haruki received the pile of papers in the mail on a morning of false apocalyptic hues several weeks before being approached on the subway by a strange and fascinating woman, and, because she was strange, all the more fascinating.

He didn't know what to do with the papers, but nonetheless a voice right above his shoulder, close to his ear with perfumed breath, whispered to him: go and take the small book that lies open in the hands of the angel who is standing on the sea and on the land.

The prophet of the apocalypse took the book and swallowed it. In his mouth it was like sweet honey but it turned his stomach sour.

But Haruki thought it better to leave that mystery alone. He still, on that day now past, needed to finish some illustrations due to another publisher that should have been finished weeks before. He had been illustrating books for twenty years and they all knew that he worked slowly. They even gave him generous deadlines; for that reason he felt particularly bad when he couldn't meet them. But that always happened.

He left the papers inside the envelope. He left the envelope on top of the sofa, like someone who couldn't care less. He would see to them later.

Much later, when it was already night, it finally started pouring. Haruki decided to sit at his worktable, in front of the window that at that hour revealed only the flooded darkness outside. The world hissed like hot oil in a skillet. The rain was so imposing that it seemed to hold everything else in suspension.

In his watercolor a crystallized snowflake appeared. Haruki had never seen snow. It was not part of the climatic vocabulary of the few cities in which he had lived. He dug at the tip of the snowflake with the tip of his paintbrush. He didn't need to experience things directly. He could simply draw them, that was experience enough. Therefore he could create snow in the tropics, at the end of spring. An indestructible snowflake. Something that circulated within the territory of hope and challenge.

His family name, Ishikawa, was composed of two unimportant ideograms: 石川. That he knew. The first, made with five strokes, signified stone. The second, made with three, signified river. An inheritance left by the senior Ishikawa: the fragile idea of a river flowing over silent stones, merely passing through a world of dreams.

Haruki was aware that a river spoke of doubts. It is restless and ever changing. It could never crystallize on the stones that welcomed it. At the same time, the stones, which seemed to be eternal, could wear down and become dislocated in the most poignant manner of all—without show or warning. The river and the stone, which Haruki had inherited from his father in his name, were things that seriously contradicted one another.

JUNE 19TH (*Afternoon*)

I take up the book. Bashō's diary in Saga. It is ten after five, a bright, humid afternoon. Alone, I see Kyoto from the heights. Someplace, in the northwest of this city, lies Rakushisha, the Hut of Fallen Persimmons.

I put the music that Haruki gave me as a present, before leaving for Tokyo, on the small CD player. Gagaku. Which in Japanese, according to the CD insert, means elegant, correct, or refined music.

There is no maestro conducting the orchestra. The musicians follow the beat of the drum.

Held by a magnet on the refrigerator door are the instructions for recycling. On the sink, the cucumbers and the tomatoes, the apples, the mushrooms, and the garlic. The people who previously lived in this apartment left things behind, and this small space is also a point of convergence in the world, a palimpsest of the people who have passed through, but who wanted to sign the affidavit of their passage with a courtesy or two.

They left behind a coffee filter. Only two, but identical, wine glasses. Mismatching plates, tea cups ditto. A trace of fabric softener and some dishwashing liquid. A rice cooker.

I take up Bashō's diary, the translation of which Haruki is preparing to illustrate and which was the motive of his trip to Japan. I read:

IN THE FOURTH YEAR OF GENROKU, JUNIOR FIRE AND RAM, ON THE EIGHTEENTH DAY OF THE FOURTH LUNAR MONTH, I TRAVEL TO SAGA TO THE HOUSE OF KYORAI, TO HIS HUT OF FALLEN PERSIMMONS. BONCHŌ, WHO ACCOMPANIES ME, RETURNS TO KYOTO AS EVENING FALLS. AS FOR MYSELF, WHO PLAN TO REMAIN FOR A LONGER PERIOD, THEY HAVE GIVEN ME A ROOM IN A CORNER OF THE HOUSE, WHERE THE PAPER WALL PARTITIONS HAVE BEEN REPAIRED AND THE GARDEN HAS BEEN WEEDED. THERE THEY HAVE PREPARED A WORKTABLE AND A BOOKSHELF WITH THE COLLECTIONS OF *Hakushishū* AND *Honchō ichinin isshu, Yotsugi monogatari, The Tale of Genji, Tosa Nikki,* AND *Shōyōshū.* IN A FIVE-TIERED LACQUER BOX, PAINTED WITH GOLD POWDER IN THE CHINESE FASHION, THEY HAVE PLACED SEVERAL TYPES OF SWEETS, AS WELL AS A BOTTLE OF THE FINEST SAKÉ AND WINE CUPS. BED LINENS, AS WELL AS DIVERSE OTHER AMENITIES, HAVE BEEN BROUGHT HERE FROM KYOTO, AND I WANT FOR NOTHING. I FORGET MY POVERTY AND FULLY APPRECIATE THIS PEACEFUL COMFORT.

The papers inside the envelope. The envelope on top of the sofa.
All of Haruki's work as an artist and book illustrator was carefully impregnated by an image, an idea, of something very vague called Brazil, half Amazonic, partly coastal, invaded by scenery from within and by his desire to capture with his eyes a ground composed of many, woven together within the same frontiers, a group of conjoined twins united here by their hands, there by their stomachs, and over there by a fragile strand of hair.

In his arsenal of visual metaphors, Haruki pictured a Brazil of jaboticaba and jaracatiá fruits, babassu palm trees, ingá vines and curiola, immense jatobá trees, animals, faces, laces, colors, industrial pollution, gold-grass baskets, children with swollen bellies, scowling figureheads on the river boats, soccer balls made of socks, slab rooftops and kites, river waters, folkloric headless mules and black-faced steer, mangrove waters, houses on stilts, ocean waters, brush fires, pampas, illegal logging, forests named loneliness.

And all of a sudden, at the drop of a hat, his publisher got in touch: We're going to publish one of the Japanese poet Bashō's diaries. The translator, Yukiko Sakade, suggested your name for the illustrations. We thought that was a great idea.

A great idea! Not for him, Haruki. It was for someone who was familiar with the subject. Someone who would draw a cherry tree in bloom instead of a jatobá tree. A little samurai instead of a barefoot boy.

But an instant of silence—words can also fly away, and he was unable to catch them quickly enough—was all that his publisher needed to win the jackpot. I'll send you the originals. You take a look, we'll talk later.

The papers inside the envelope. The envelope on top of the sofa.

The translator, Yukiko Sakade, suggested your name for the illustrations.

And so what if he went to Japan? That is what occurred to him days later. A strange idea and Exceedingly Adventurous. Haruki wasn't like that. Simply thinking of the length of the flight made him feel like backing out. But just when he would feel like that, the idea would grab hold of the world, it would bite into Haruki's sleep, the category of Exceedingly Adventurous things would loosen up, it would grow weak in the knees, relax between the letters of the words, give way.

No links with the country of his ancestors. Nothing. No information, no curiosity.

Someone once commented to Haruki that it was very rare to associate Brazilians with Asian features, you rarely saw those features in people on the soap operas, people on TV, people in the fashion industry, people on stage, in the gossip magazines.

Haruki shrugged; he couldn't care less about those Asian features. Not even his own mirror remembered them.

Japan was just another country in the world, perched on land that had been there since the times in which the gods Izanami and Izanagi had poked at the lower regions of the sky and watched as the ocean water that dripped off the tips of their spears congealed into the island of Onogoro. Resting on such legends, repeated during Haruki's childhood, that seemed neither more nor less interesting than others of other foreign nations. Japan had nothing to do with his life and his slanted eyes.

Until the day he met that girl. Yukiko Sakade. The translator.

But she had come and gone like a traveling salesman, leaving a hole with the diameter of a year in his life.

Yes, she was of Japanese descent. And that—nothing more than a coincidence. The world was full of them—women of Japanese descent, translators, coincidences.

And now he wasn't sleepy. He put aside his blunt pencil and the paper. It had been quite some time that the human voices within his thoughts had been silenced. The world no longer spoke a specific language. Everything was very far away from there.

Very far. If life could only bend just once, and then once again, and once more, successively, for all eternity, surfaces could be more easily disguised. There would be deep curves where you could hide to wait for sleep to come, to peek at death. There would be breaches, like the dens of distrustful animals, where you could repair your dreams, where you could patch the clothes of your official life, at the places worn bare by longing. There would be a way to look at longing in the eyes without awakening the dragon that lay within. There would be spaces, alcoves, drawers in which you could keep secrets inside of old magazines, wilted petals of the briefest of flowers pressed between the yellowed pages of books often read.

There would be lapses in which the creator of that false angel of the apocalypse would give in to daydreaming, and the latent gestures would come out, breaking the skin of existence. Assuring. Assuring yourself. There would be a way of legitimizing anything that opposes the laws of multiple proportions, of gravity, of planetary motion, of electrodynamics, of conservation, of inertia.

There would be a way of forever keeping a person in your arms on a specific night and on the following nights, too few, insufficient nights, keep that person in the coziness of pillows and covers in the pulsating interior of a bedroom, within the disguise of four walls.

Within the desire a carpet of materiality would be spread out. No angel of the apocalypse, true or false, would come to disturb you, because the angels would be right there and they would be of flesh, bones, and sex, with their wings folded, capable of achieving the inverted fall: from hell to heaven.

In Tokyo, far from everything, alone, Haruki slowly fell asleep. There was a silence inside of him, and that silence was ever broader.

Celina

Hordes of Japanese students were going up and down the streets of Higashiyama. Celina had come on foot from Karasuma Station, on the other side of the Kamo River. It was already a familiar route, after three weeks. Downtown Kyoto. She would go down Shijō Street, the busy commercial zone, the large department stores, she would cross the bridge and wander through the Gion alleyways, where she might sometimes see the maiko, the apprentice geisha.

How was it possible that she felt at home there, if she could not even understand the inscriptions on the signs around her? If she could make no sense of the words being said around her?

But it was a home. It was a safe home. There was nothing to fear in Kyoto, in the solitude she felt in Kyoto, her friendly companion solitude. She walked along the cobblestone streets: Ninenzaka and Sannenzaka. If she were to slip and fall there, as legend had it, she would have two or three years of bad luck, respectively.

Two, three years—what was that? An abstraction. Numbers. Two years equaled seven hundred and thirty and one-half days. That's one-fiftieth of a century. That's one five-hundredth of a millennium. In two years the earth rotated twice around the sun, tracing its ellipse, indifferent to all the names it is given. What silly things to think, thought Celina.

She observed the young women in high heels balancing themselves on the cobblestones. They all seemed to be so weightless, as if they were floating a short distance above the ground, and their skin always so fair. The numerous girls that were in fashion overdid their makeup. Their hair was long and shaggy and sometimes blond.

Eventually Celina arrived at the Yasaka Kōshindō, a small temple dedicated to the Buddhist guardian Kōshin-san. There were dozens and more dozens of small colorful cloth bundles hanging there. She approached. She picked up a small brochure for tourists, in English. The small bundles were not bundles, but representations of Kukurizaru, the monkey, which with its hands and feet tied together could not move.

Rid yourself of one of your desires to have a wish granted. Place this desire in Kukurizaru, and the guardian Kōshin-san will help you control it. If your desire tries to escape, join your hands together and recite the Buddhist sutra: *on deiba yakisha banda banda kakakaka sowaka.*

There were children playing in front of the small temple. Celina entered one of the handicraft shops.

While Marco was taking a shower, on the first afternoon they spent together, she lay in bed humming "Peter Gast": I can fly and my muscles are tensed. Then he said: You were singing to me. And she: No I was not.

She also often sang "Peter Gast" while she rocked newborn Alice, intermingling Caetano Veloso's song with traditional lullabies. No one is ordinary and I am no one.

Alice who was a night owl and slept all day. Alice who seemed to have unusually large eyes and was born with those two enormous black spheres wide open, ready for the world.

In the handicraft shop in Higashiyama they had zori, sandals with rush weed straps, the soles shaped like wedges. Several sizes. Some of those sandals would fit Alice. She would also like the tabi, socks divided at the big toe, made especially for zori, and for the geta, clogs made of wood, very high.

Somewhere Celina had read that centuries ago women used geta as high as seven inches. She looked down at her own feet. How could it be possible to walk like that, with seven inches between your skin and the ground.

Celina tried to explain the size of the sandals to the saleswoman. She tried to explain that they were not for herself, but for a seven-year-old child.

The saleswoman called a small girl who was seated in a corner, petting a white cat. Celina looked at the girl's feet.

Hai—a word she now knew to mean yes—more or less her size.

At the beginning of her pregnancy, Marco was sick along with her. Sometimes he was so nervous he would simultaneously have morning sickness. Celina would smile and stroke his hair and they would end up in bed and he would say they needed to be careful of the baby.

And then— and then—and then. To learn to walk again as Alice had learned to walk one day, when she was eleven months old, breaking in her bones, muscles, tendons. The streets that Celina trod could bring an indefinite period of bad luck were she to fall. All of the streets. All of the sidewalks, staircases, bridges, subway platforms.

What a mystery to be there, in Kyoto, thinking about Alice. A tangible, visible mystery, a dragonfly mystery beating its small wings in the infinity of the air. Stirring up images, smells, memories, ideas, wishes, shaking up the universe with the almost nonexistent oscillation of its fragile wings.

What a mystery to be there in Kyoto, thinking about Marco. A concrete, sensitive mystery, a mystery that grabbed her by the neck and launched her into the infinite air. To have severed all the links, the ties, everything that led to him. Except for the heartache. The memory of having one day fallen down, in the street that would bring her more bad luck. Of having shattered the mirror. Of having invoked despair in the oscillation of the fragile dragonfly wings.

Celina left the handicraft shop with her bag. It wouldn't get dark for quite a while. She could still walk in the daylight. And walk, and walk. Go up the steep alleyways to Kiyomizudera, the Pure Water Temple, twelve centuries old, visited by multitudes of students in search of the best angle for taking photographs. All of the groups, all of them, Celina verified, made a V with their index and middle fingers as they posed. Like the old hippie love and peace. The shopping bag with the pair of zori swung in Celina's fingers, back, and forth, back, and forth.

June 20th

Coming back home from Kiyomizudera, I came across this incense shop. I don't know how long I stayed in there. They had so many types of incense, sticks and wood chips and cones and spirals. I read that it has been a Kyoto specialty for centuries. I read that the art of incense here is as traditional as ikebana floral arrangements or tea ceremonies.

There was something written on the package of the incense

that I had decided to buy. I asked the saleswoman what it said. She didn't speak English.

Mukashi, mukashi, she said, reading the words on the package. Mukashi, mukashi. She made gestures with her hand to indicate times past.

Mukashi mukashi is how they often begin stories in Japan. Mukashi, mukashi—a long time ago. The incense that I bought was an aroma inspired by a book.

I lit the incense and put it into a pinecone I had picked up off the street. I turned on the television and flipped through half a dozen channels. I turned off the television. I remembered Marco and the day that I removed the path that led from the world to Marco. A silence of the dead on the fields of battle. A hue of dried blood. Amputated arms. Blank eyes. A ghost passes through the bodies without touching the ground.

Mukashi, mukashi—a long time ago.

The incense was green and the smoke began to slowly spread throughout the living room. I thought of its trajectory in my body. From my nostrils into my lungs. I wondered if my blood would inhale that incense smoke and take it to my cells. If my cells would nestle in the sweet and good Kyoto incense.

JUNE 20TH (*Very Late at Night*)

I didn't know what to expect when we landed in Japan. We changed planes in Amsterdam. I had never left my country. I had never had much money nor much desire for that. Perhaps I'd never intended to leave. Never, during all my life (this adventure of an indefinite duration that springs trapdoors on us).

Why had I said yes to Haruki's invitation? Could it have been for the novelty of it, and for the beauty of his face at the taxi door on São Clemente Street, as he looked off into the illuminated night of Rio?

I never imagined I would take my savings and spend them on a Rio–Amsterdam–Osaka–Amsterdam–Rio airplane ticket.

But what difference does it make, to have or not to have savings. If I had any, it was purely by chance. They weren't for anything. They certainly weren't for my old age, nor to buy a car or make a down payment on a piece of property, nor for the possibility of an illness. Those things are ridiculously tenuous attempts to provide for the future. I don't believe in them. Those things, I realize today, only serve to give a name to hope. They are intended for those who hope for something.

My country was getting farther and farther away. My language. Suddenly Latin faces disappeared, they went on from Amsterdam to other destinations, and I became a disparity. No more Portuguese speakers in the vicinity.

Our plane flew over Russia and landed in Osaka on a bright summer morning. I had been traveling for so many hours and through so many time zones that my body felt suspended, as if I didn't really exist. I kept getting cramps in my feet. I could no longer imagine if I should be asleep or awake, having lunch or dinner, if I should be hungry or not.

There was transportation waiting to take us to Kyoto, a little over an hour away. A van with an impeccably dressed driver, white gloves and a cap. The car seats lined with white lace, white and clean. Other passengers who had arrived in Osaka and who, like us, had Kyoto as their final destination. A new car, a perfect highway, ditto for the signs, the motor purring and the wheels turning almost imperceptibly.

The passenger in front of me spoke English. She turned

around to translate information that the driver was giving, in Japanese, over the loudspeaker. Not that we had asked anything. It was the first demonstration of that consideration with which the Kyoto inhabitants would continually surprise me, in the weeks to come. An almost nervous, an almost anxious consideration. A miracle.

When we got into town, I was thirsty. I asked her if there was anything to drink in the van. Worried, she exchanged a few words in a low voice with an older woman next to her. She turned back to me and said no. But the van could stop at a gas station, we could buy something. That's not necessary, I said. I'll soon be home. Home, I said.

She and the woman next to her—her mother?—got out before we did, in front of a small house with narrow strips of land on either side, minute lots, with rice planted. One of them quickly entered the house while the other helped the driver unload the suitcases.

Before we left, the older Japanese woman came back to the van with four small brown bags. She gave one to me, one to Haruki, one to the other passenger, and one to the driver.

I opened it. There was a bottle of iced green tea (like the ones widely available in Japan in vending machines, as I would discover in the following days) and a package of cookies.

There was a certain afternoon, a specific afternoon, that Celina would always remember. It was as if it had remained highlighted among the other images that had peacefully yielded to forgetfulness. That afternoon did not appear to be willing to succumb.

There was nothing that special about it. Perhaps for that

reason. An afternoon that shied away from a celebrity label. With no pretensions whatsoever, no demands.

The three of them and the Lagoa in Rio. Celina, Marco, and Alice. A few cormorants nearby. People passing by, not many.

Rio de Janeiro was just a city that had recuperated its axis of lethargy. Just a city, without subtitles, without being the capital of anything, not of beauty, nor of poverty, nor of fear, nor of drug traffic wars, nor of Carnival, just a city momentarily made small. Of dozing masks. Saint Sebastian without the arrows.

At the edge of the Lagoa, the three of them: mother, father, small daughter sleeping in her buggy. None of them particularly beautiful, particularly happy or unhappy, simply walking while, around them, the cormorants were landing and taking flight.

Marco and Celina sat down on a bench. He pulled the buggy closer to himself. Alice slept with her mouth slightly agape and a strand of saliva trickled from between her plump lips, forming a small, humid stain on her pillow. Celina lay down on the bench still warm from the sun that had just set. Her head on Marco's thigh. Her forehead frowning up at the bright sky and her eyes following a cormorant.

So easy. So frightfully easy, she would think, later, when nothing could ever go back to being easy, when nothing could ever again include Marco and Alice—and that afternoon clung to her memory as if it were an insult.

Alice

They removed her training wheels early on. Alice didn't need them anymore. Before she knew how to read or write she was familiar with pedals and balance, she liked speed. After half a dozen spills, she learned to trust space.

A small price to pay. Half a dozen spills in exchange for riding all over the place.

There was that long dirt road near her grandmother's house, in the countryside. Alice wasn't allowed to go out by herself. An adult, or an older child, would go along. Alice pedaled and the tires grated against the small stones along the way. The road became bumpier and bumpier as the months went by. The rainy season dug pits in the ground and created mud holes. Now and again, but not as often as necessary, they would smooth it out with a tractor that everyone called "the machine": they ran the machine over the road.

After they ran the machine over the road near her grandmother's house, it was hard to keep Alice in check. Distances shrank. She would go buy candy several times a day, just to be able to have the pedals touch her feet and the muscles of her legs produce speed on the two wheels balanced between air and air, above the earthen ground.

She also liked to go barefoot. Her goal was to toughen the soles of her feet so that she would never need shoes. She sometimes exercised: She would walk on top of small hard stones, which caused her shooting pain. Walk on the hot ground beneath the sun at high noon. Every day she would make a bit more progress. She would then feel the roughness of her feet with her hands, the tiny cracks on her heels, and evaluate her secret project.

She had heard that girls should have smooth feet. She regarded her mother's polished toenails and groomed feet. How silly.

It was good to feel her bare feet on the bicycle pedals. She pedaled strongly and felt the metal against her skin as she felt the wind that she herself had created.

JUNE 21ST

Haruki slept a long time our first afternoon in Kyoto. He was exhausted. I'm not sure whether he had managed to get much sleep on the plane. He watched a few films. He said that one of them was *The Godfather*. He got up several times.

I found the pale late spring sky odd and at any moment expected the promised rainy season—which however, against all expectations, would not come all that soon. It would only rain for the first time in earnest after Haruki went to Tokyo. I didn't know the meaning of the labels of the products that by and by I ferreted out of the cupboards, in the apartment. I tried to discover what things were by their smell.

He slept, our first afternoon in this city. At that moment he was no one, he wasn't even himself, he was more of a reconstruction. A novel. A piece of fiction behind closed eyes. Was there a heartache hidden away someplace? Does everyone have a heartache hidden away someplace? And if they do, how big might it be?

How do you measure pain? Are there personal units? Cubic inches, meters, acres? And could pain go away? Would pain simply rain during the right season, that here they call tsuyu, the rainy season, a nightmare at the beginning of the summer? And would the dampness of pain evaporate beneath a sun full of promise?

I went out for a walk, while he slept, on that first afternoon. Outside I saw boys in their uniforms for a baseball game, after school. They were all thin and lanky, their blue-and-white uniforms spotless. I also began to feel sleepy. It was twelve hours later in my body. At home, in Rio, it would be a little after five in the morning.

When I returned, Haruki was still asleep.

Looking at him, I vaguely thought of sex, the sex that had not taken place between us. I think I giggled. The two of us were there, between four walls, we had come halfway around the world together.

I stayed where I was. I closed the door so that the sounds I was making in the living room wouldn't disturb him. Even though I didn't know yet how much noises might or might not disturb his sleep.

Could I possibly ask him to give me a script, something like a tourist guide of himself?

A manual. Appropriate phrases to say for each situation. His party colors and his mourning colors. Arrows indicating directions.

The consequences of internal wars. The prerogatives of power.

I now wonder if I should have gone with Haruki to Tokyo.
Company. Friendship. Sex. Hands to tie up. Futures to pretend.
Maybe yes, maybe no. I pick up the pages of the translation he
left me and I once more encounter the poet Bashō.

19th day

AT APPROXIMATELY TWELVE-THIRTY, WE VISIT THE RINSEN
TEMPLE. THE ŌI RIVER FLOWS IN FRONT, AND TO THE RIGHT
RISES MOUNT ARASHI, IMMEDIATELY BEHIND THE VILLAGE
OF MATSUNOŌ. THERE IS A GREAT AMOUNT OF ACTIVITY AS
PILGRIMS GO BACK AND FORTH TO WORSHIP KOKŪZŌ. IN THE
BAMBOO GROVES OF MATSUNOŌ LIES THE SUPPOSED RESI-
DENCE OF LADY KOGŌ, WHICH MAKES THREE—WITH THE
ONE TO THE NORTH AND THE OTHER ONE TO THE SOUTH OF
SAGA. WHICH IS THE AUTHENTIC ONE? SINCE THIS ONE LIES
CLOSE TO THE PLACE WHERE THEY SAY THE FAMOUS
NAKAKUNI REINED IN HIS HORSE, AND WHICH IS CALLED THE
BRIDGE OF THE HORSE'S PAUSE, PERHAPS IT IS THE TRUE
SITE. LADY KOGŌ'S TOMB LIES NEAR A TEAHOUSE AMONGST
THE BAMBOO. THEY PLANTED A CHERRY TREE TO MARK THE
SPOT. WITH DUE RESPECT, THAT LADY LIVED HER DAYS OUT
CLOTHED IN BROCADES AND DAMASKS, BUT AT THE END SHE
TURNED TO DUST IN THE MIDST OF CRAWLING PLANTS. I
EVOKE THE LEGENDS OF ANCIENT TIMES—THE WILLOWS OF
THE VILLAGE OF ZHAOJUN AND THE SHRINE FLOWERS.

MERCILESS DESTINY

IT WAS HER FATE

TO BECOME A BAMBOO SHOOT

uki fushi ya

take no ko to naru

hito no hate

AT MOUNT ARASHI

THE WIND WEAVES THROUGH

DENSE BAMBOO GROVE

Arashiyama

yabu no shigeri ya

kaze no suji

WHEN THE SUN BEGINS TO SET ON THE HORIZON, WE
RETURN TO THE HUT OF FALLEN PERSIMMONS. BONCHŌ
ARRIVES FROM KYOTO. KYORAI RETURNS TO KYOTO. I RETIRE
TO BED AS SOON AS NIGHT FALLS.

There were three wilted roses in the vase. Marco had arrived from
the Sunday street market with those three roses. One yellow, two
red. Three roses in addition to three papayas and some small,
acidic apples, the kind Celina liked, and persimmons for Alice.
And a bunch of spinach.

In the afternoon Alice went to the beach with a family friend.
They took their bicycles. Her nine-year-old friend filled Alice with
pride because she had just turned seven and she always felt privileged to be around older children. Her friend was two inches
taller. Alice looked up at those inches above her own and felt
something bordering on adoration.

At home the three roses emitted a sweet aroma. Celina was
asleep when Marco went to the bedroom. The window was open,
and the air, almost motionless, barely stirred the curtains. The

afternoon light was bright and filled the room, but Celina slept, her pale body on top of the colorful spread, her bare legs, her almost childlike plain white panties, her almost worn-out red T-shirt.

Marco lay down next to her. He looked at Celina without haste.

What would you do, Celina had asked him the night before, if it were your last day with me?

The night before, he had raised his eyes to her and smiled. What a thought.

It's that I'm reading this book here, she explained. A last day, and they both know it, because she's leaving, and there's nothing he can do about it.

He could go with her.

No, not in this case he can't.

Are you thinking about leaving?

She smiled, tossed her head, and lowered her eyes back to her book.

Then he remembered: what he would do if it was his last day with that woman who had the same eyes as his daughter.

Celina's eyes were closed. Asleep. Marco slowly reached his hand out to her breast, under her shirt. He sought out her nipple. She rose out of her sleep almost imperceptibly, without a sound, just barely fluttering her shoulders. She slowly opened her eyes and looked for Marco. He looked at her. Close your eyes, he said.

He pulled her T-shirt up. The breasts that he knew. The nipples that he knew, with that color, with that consistency, with that taste. Marco slid the shirt off her arms, off her hands. Then he joined Celina's two wrists together next to the headboard of the bed. He stretched the T-shirt out and began to tie her up, slowly, with patience and gentleness, because, after all, even if it were the last day on earth, there would be no reason to rush.

She opened her eyes. Close your eyes, he said. Pull your arms down, he said. She lightly pulled on them. Harder, he said. She pulled harder. She couldn't break loose.

Marco ran his hands down over her breasts, then ran them down her whole body until he lay on Celina's closed legs. He held them with force. He embraced them. Try to open your legs, he said. She tried. He squeezed harder.

He slid his mouth over her joined thighs and down to her feet. Her toes, there on the edge of sleep, were almost fragile. Slowly, he let his tongue occupy the small space between the toes, one by one. As if he were measuring the size of those minute valleys. Slowly he enveloped, one by one, her toes with his mouth. From her feet he returned to her ankles and to her knees and to her thighs. With his free hand he gently pulled down her white panties.

Just look what I found.

And his finger tracing almost imperceptible circular movements at a small spot between her closed legs.

Do you suppose that this is what I would do if it were our last day?

In the living room the sweet roses, three of them.

And at the beach, the salty breeze tangling Alice's hair, which she liked to let grow very long like that of her nine-year-old friend. She could feel the moisture like a whip on her face—the air, the wind, the ocean spray.

Kyoto Station was a place that Celina liked. The swarms of people did not intimidate her. She had read that it was one of the largest buildings in Japan. She liked the great staircase with the nearly two hundred steps. The futuristic façade, with its surface of irregularly shaped glass. The countless floors with shops, movie theaters, the Isetan department store, and all arranged somehow in an inexplicably organic arrangement, including the basement.

Sometimes Haruki and Celina would get lost there, in search of a specific spot that seemed to disappear in a sea of people, of stores, of food, of clothes racks.

Celina went with Haruki to the station the day he took the Shinkansen, the bullet train, to Tokyo, to search for the memory of the poet Matsuo Bashō: Nozomi, the fastest train of all, which sped at 185 miles per hour.

Haruki was quiet. They sat down for a cup of tea in a place chosen haphazardly. To while away the time.

Haruki bought donuts from a Western chain. They were too sweet. But that's how they taste, Celina said. They're sweets that are too sweet. They tickle my throat.

It had been a week since Haruki and Celina had arrived in Kyoto. He then decided to go to Tokyo, and from there perhaps farther north. If he had come this far, he wanted to go even farther. One possible idea: visit Sendai, the land of his father's family?

It would make you happy, old man. Nudge the past with the tip of my toe. To prove its immobility?

Capture images along the road with his eyes, his best photographic camera (but he had the other kind, just in case). Let Bashō's land penetrate his five senses, let it nestle in his lungs, imprint itself onto his fingerprints, undulate in green tea on his tongue (even if accompanied by donuts), let a great Zen temple bell resonate in his ears, even if mixed in with the profuse and distinct timbres of cell phones.

Above all let Bashō's land engrave itself onto his eyes and onto the memory of his eyes, even though it be amidst the often-criticized visual pollution of modern-day Japan. See the frog leap in Bashō's old pond, listen to the faint murmur of the water, and then observe the concentric circles spread out and disappear. Almost a dream. Almost real life.

To Tokyo, without Celina, who preferred to remain in Kyoto.

Haruki was still wondering what it was that Celina had found in Kyoto. And what it was that Celina had found within her heart to come with him, such a preposterous acceptance of a preposterous invitation, two negatives together have always resulted in and always will result in a third negative.

If she was running away, or simply running, or running to the aid of someone, or to their assistance, or forgetting, or remembering, if she was closing her eyes, if she was opening them.

The illustrator and the girl who made cloth purses sleeping in the same bed for a week. It was like this: Fully dressed, they each grabbed a pillow. A blanket for each one of them.

There was that night that they looked at each other more than usual. The lamps on the night stands were turned on. Celina was reading. Haruki was looking at brochures that he had picked up that day. And when she closed the book and turned toward him— it was the moment when they were closest to that silent place where things without names can happen.

They exchanged glances as if their bodies were ready. And simply didn't know how to proceed, how to make the metamorphosis from the sense of sight to the sense of touch.

The crickets were singing outside. The insects of forgetfulness.

Their bodies stayed where they were and the lights remained lit for a few more minutes. Finally words emerged through Celina's lips. They tore away from her moist skin, grazed her teeth, and succeeded: It's beautiful, the book, she said. And somewhere an extremely fragile hope was destroyed.

Flee from what. As if flight were possible. Only in the musical sense, perhaps, as in Bach's fugues, in which one voice pursued the other, and their paths appeared to obtain autonomy, but they then come together in the final chord. Haruki knew how to play Bach's fugues on the piano, although it had been years since he had been near the instrument. Could he still? Produce melodies that misled and searched out each other, like lovers in an erotic game? And what would Bach think of that, erotic games—he, a man of god? Was it possible to divide the corporeal from the spiritual, or did they both (erotically) overlap, like the melodic overlap, like the melodic line of a fugue? But one's spirit, Haruki thought, lived in the nerve cells, and the body was a volatile substance, like alcohol—it just took slightly longer to become volatile.

And would it ever be possible to lead the heart away from the melodic line of one's thoughts? Haruki had an intuition about Celina. Perhaps for that reason he had not gotten closer to her beyond a certain sound barrier.

The truth of the matter, he was intuitive.

Not so long ago, he had had an intuition about the silence in another woman. First he had intuited happiness, like this: how could it be anything less than written, maktub, in all the stars? Afterward that beloved woman went back to her own and other life, that beloved woman and her wedding band, totally consistent with her left hand, that questionable testament of another bond, and Haruki sensed the necessary silence of a last afternoon in which the only thing uttered was that it was raining hard outside.

From that invisible woman, from that volatile body that evaporated when the sun came out to shine again, he saved an alarming number of sketches. For an entire year, he thought that she would appear in everything that he could imagine. The point of his pencils, the tip of his paintbrushes, there she was, always—and the publishers thinking that he was really illustrating the stories that they had sent him, when all he was doing was crying out in colors the loss of being separated from what he most desired. From whom he most desired. He felt that he was monothematic at an embarrassing level, in the survival of his sketches. So be it. Until whenever it might be. The double melodic line until the final chord.

Yukiko was her name. The translator. Yukiko had brought Bashō with her, and that Japanese inconsistency that was in Haruki himself in spite of his father and his physical features and everything else. And the publisher talking about a challenge and blah blah blah.

This is the challenge. In his seat on the bullet train between Kyoto and Tokyo. There must be a way to get lost, some way or another. There must be a way to get lost in order to find some place on earth where no one has tread, a truly virgin territory. There must be a way, who knows, to take off on a trip and never come back. Limit yourself to a backpack and a few changes of clothes. Limit yourself, or expand yourself, to an absence of your own house and citizenship, crumple up the flypaper of everyday life and transform it, everyday life, into an infinitely movable adventure. Movable. Unglue it from the ground. Lift your feet to walk, study your compass and your maps, but make all gestures random. Draw a straight line, the shortest distance between two points, and cut it up into small pieces with a pair of scissors, eradicate parts of it with an eraser, disguise other parts with a blending stump, take it off its tracks with curves. So that it might one day forget that it was a straight line, endowed with an endpoint. With an objective. Strip it of its objective. That would be truly virgin territory—the only one. To find meaning in the lack of any meaning in life. In all of its possible meanings.

He had an intuition about Celina. Some sort of silence as well, which now separated them: after having come halfway around the world, he was leaving, she was staying. At home, in Kyoto, that seemed to be home without any possibility of being so, and perhaps precisely for that reason.

Bashō

JUNE 22ND

I went out for an excursion with Bashō. I placed the loose pages into my purse. I decided to go to Tetsugaku no michi, the Philosopher's Walk. I got off at Keage Station and memorized the name in Japanese: Tetsugaku no michi? was what I asked the occasional passerby.

Lovely, considerate faces gave me directions that I did not understand, but their hand gestures indicated the direction that I should take. I followed the smiles. I am following the smiles of the inhabitants of Kyoto. They give me a north. They grant me authenticity. I sit on a bench and take the pages out of my purse.

20th day

THE NUN UKŌ ARRIVES TO SEE THE FESTIVAL OF THE NORTH OF SAGA. KYORAI COMES FROM KYOTO AND RECITES A POEM WRITTEN ALONG THE ROAD:

> BICKERING CHILDREN
>
> THE HEIGHT OF
>
> BARLEY IN THE FIELDS

tsukamiau

kodomo no take ya

mugibatake

THE HUT OF FALLEN PERSIMMONS IS THE SAME AS WHEN
BUILT BY THE FORMER OWNER, BUT ITS DETERIORATION CAN BE
SEEN ALL ABOUT. ITS WOEFUL STATE MOVES ME MORE THAN IF
IT WERE NEW. THE CARVED WOODEN BEAMS AND THE WALL
MURALS HAVE BEEN DEVASTATED BY THE WIND AND SOAKED BY
THE RAIN. UNUSUAL ROCKS AND ODDLY SHAPED TREES LIE
BENEATH THE OVERRUN VINES. FACING THE BAMBOO VERANDA
IS A LONE LEMON TREE, WITH FRAGRANT FLOWERS.

LEMON BLOSSOMS—
I SHALL REMEMBER OLDEN DAYS
AND THE KITCHEN

yu no hana ya
mukashi shinobamu
ryōri no ma

A CUCKOO;
THE GREAT BAMBOO GROVES
FILTER THE MOONLIGHT

hototogisu
ōtakeyabu o moru
tsukiyo

THE NUN UKŌ:

I SHALL RETURN
WHEN AGAIN RIPEN
STRAWBERRIES ON MOUNT SAGA

mata ya kon

ichigo akarame

Saga no yama

THE WIFE OF KYORAI'S OLDEST BROTHER HAS SENT US SWEETS
AND DELICACIES. THIS EVENING, LADY UKŌ STAYS WITH US,
TOTALING FIVE PEOPLE BENEATH A SINGLE MOSQUITO NET. IT
IS DIFFICULT TO FALL ASLEEP AND AFTER MIDNIGHT WE ALL
ARISE, SO WE TAKE OUTSIDE WITH US THE SWEETS AND THE
GLASSES OF SAKÉ LEFT FROM THE AFTERNOON AND TALK UNTIL
MORNING. LAST SUMMER, WHEN BONCHŌ SLEPT AT MY HOUSE,
WE WERE FOUR PEOPLE FROM FOUR DIFFERENT PROVINCES,
SLEEPING UNDER THE SAME MOSQUITO NET. "FOUR MINDS AND
THEREFORE FOUR DIFFERENT TYPES OF DREAMS," SOMEONE
SAID, IN JEST, AND WE ALL LAUGHED. COME MORNING, UKŌ
AND BONCHŌ RETURN TO KYOTO, AND KYORAI STAYS.

To reach the Philosopher's Walk, I went through Nanzenji. I made
a mental note: come back to this temple on another day, at
another moment. And I continued to ask: Tetsugaku no michi?

Emphatic gestures and words that I did not understand tried
to help me. I vaguely understood which direction I should take. It
looked as though it might rain. I finally memorized the graphics of
the name and managed to follow the signs by myself: 哲学の道

(I later untangled the graphics. It took me quite a while on the
internet. And I came across some other information, that the Japanese language uses five different systems of writing. The kanji,
which we call ideograms but which are, literally, Chinese characters that have been imported into Japan. Two writing syllabaries,
hiragana and katakana, the second used above all for Western
words. Romaji, Latin characters. And also Indo-Arabic numerals.)

It was hot. It showered briefly for ten minutes, no longer. I stopped to eat an ice cream with a bean sweet. It came with fruit and cubes of transparent gelatin. I didn't eat the gelatin.

I sat there, alone in the shelter of the small teahouse, watching the rain dampen the asphalt. The sky soon cleared up, totally blue. Tall blond tourists passed by on rented bicycles and in rickshaws guided by thin, strong Japanese men.

I'm under the impression that all the Japanese are thin. I must have written this before. They always seem about to levitate, as if they barely touch the ground, with an elegance that would be impossible for a Westerner. Next to them I feel excessive, brutish, clumsy.

But I have tried to treat objects with the reverence that they seem to deserve here.

That custom of taking off your shoes when entering a temple, or a home, which is a temple as well: with restraint, carefully. Never conspicuously. Shoes are removed neither quickly nor slowly, simply in the proper amount of time with the proper movements. They are placed on the ground or floor in the same fashion. I cannot imagine Japanese people tossing off their shoes any which way on the ground and barely turning back to see how they landed.

But I might be mistaken. I always could be. What do I know about the Japanese? And what could I ever expect to know, even if I actually made Kyoto my home, and stayed here for years on end or for decades?

The blond tourists on bicycles are a contrast to the young Japanese leaving school. I find them lovely, these adolescents, they give the impression of being somewhat androgynous. I like their thin bodies and their loose clothes and their intentionally mussed hair. The boys more than the girls. The girls almost always have on too much makeup, their faces look artificial. I find it amusing when they take out their colorful cell phones full of baubles and Hello Kitties. I find the entire shelves of Hello Kitty products in the stores amusing. Towels, purses, cell phone pendants, cards, all sorts of trinkets.

And at last there I was on the Philosopher's Walk, 哲学の道, which begins at the Nyakuōji Bridge and goes along the edge of the canal to the Silver Pavilion, the Ginkakuji. The walk received its name from a philosopher, Nishida Kitarō, who was one of Japan's most important philosophers and liked to stroll along there.

If I had arrived a few months earlier I would have seen the cherry trees in bloom on Nishida Kitarō's walkway. The prevalent color now is the green of the trees, there are fish in the small canal of transparent water. There are stores to one side, and to the other, tea houses, small restaurants. Cats. On the walls of the canal green moss grows between the stones.

And then the pages, a few of them, from *Saga nikki,* were guided into Haruki's hands. Yukiko, the translator, had already spoken to him of Bashō before the silence had appeared in the life—life?— that she and Haruki had had together.

An ancient poet from Japan. Nothing of particular interest to Haruki: except to the extent that everything that interested that woman was more urgent to him than hunger, than thirst, than sleep, then natural, global, planetary, interplanetary, cosmic catastrophes. His own private catastrophe.

Thus it was that Matsuo Bashō came into his life through her.

With the translation in his hands, he went to look up

something about Bashō in a book. He found what Yukiko had already told him, and more. Now she was no longer at his side for what could be long conversations that would begin in the living room, with some kind of music playing, some kind of drink and almost untouched food, and would end in a space that was an alternative to their two worlds, the interval between breathing in and breathing out, where an entire existence could fit, and where none of those things would be necessary, not clothes, nor poets, nor words.

Haruki read about that term—haiku. A poetic form. The briefest of forms, seventeen syllables, organized into three lines, in a five-seven-five format. He read that Bashō, one of the great masters among centuries of poets in Japan, was born in Iga Province, near the city of Ueno, in 1644, and died in Osaka, in the fall of 1694. But not only that, Bashō was a master of prose as well, having left behind numerous travel diaries and critical essays.

He wrote *Saga Diary* not long before he died, while staying with his disciple Kyorai at the Hut of Fallen Persimmons, on the outskirts of Kyoto. The year was 1691.

Haruki's job was to illustrate *Saga Diary.* He read and reread the diary in the translation that Yukiko had just done. That girl who wore a wedding band on her left hand, completely controversial and completely consistent.

Earlier, at the beginning of time, Haruki had intuited happiness, he had thought that it was something predestined, maktub. They both forgot about Yukiko's other lives, which were regulated by other maktubs.

Why would those stars be more privileged than the others? They were only celestial bodies without any true power over terrestrial bodies made of flesh, bones, and sex. The wingless bodies of the angels of this world, each of whom writes its own history according to where each fits in, and avoids the dizziness of abysms.

The publisher: We're going to publish one of the Japanese poet Bashō's diaries. The translator, Yukiko Sakade, suggested your name for the illustrations. We thought that was a great idea.

A possible alliance between the two, if what she wore on her left hand did not want to and could not be removed, mocked, ignored, erased, sabotaged, forgotten, melted down.

Maktub.

Only Haruki could read. Only Haruki could read the future in Yukiko's hands, in the lines of her thighs, of her feet, in the curves of her armpits, in the arabesque designs of her earlobes and sex, in the stillness of the blank page of her back.

But the illustrator did not try to make contact with the translator again. None of that hi-what-a-long-time-how-are-you. The words written in e-mails or the tone of voice on the phone could conceivably represent a newly irresistible danger. A relapse.

A relapse meant falling again. Into the bottomless well of happiness, into the renewable void of pain and refusal. Life: pay attention to the expiration date. Life: recommended dosage, consult the patient information insert. Dermatologically tested, ophthalmologically tested in torture sessions on laboratory animals. So many capsules per day, according to weight and age. In case of overdose, the stomach must be pumped. It is recommended that you consult your physician before use.

JUNE 22ND (*Night*)

The first cloth purse that I made was for Alice. We used to play at sewing together. We enjoyed going to buy the notions:

colors and textures in threads, laces, fabrics, braids, sequins, glass beads, anything that caught our eyes or felt good to the touch.

We would play at sewing with a thimble to keep from pricking our fingers. I was the one who was usually in charge of the needles. But Alice had her privileges. The first purse we finished, that we seriously finished, ended up as a lunchbox. But it didn't work out very well, everything spilled inside. But that purse led to others. Including lunchboxes lined with waterproof fabric.

Alice's best friends received purses as birthday presents, purses that took us weeks to make. It was how Alice prioritized her affections.

The zori that I bought for her are next to my suitcase. Everything is clean and straightened in this apartment. I spent the whole morning sweeping and washing. A damp cloth wiped off the dust from the furniture and electrical appliances. The food that was stuck to the pan was removed. My clothes are drying in the sun. Socks, T-shirts, panties. On top of the table rests only my diary and Bashō's diary.

21st day

HAVING SLEPT SO LITTLE LAST NIGHT, I DO NOT FEEL WELL TODAY. EVEN THE SKY IS CHANGED: OVERCAST SINCE DAWN, WITH THE OCCASIONAL SOUND OF RAIN. THROUGHOUT THE ENTIRE DAY I HAVE DOZED, HERE AND THERE. AS EVENING COMES, KYORAI RETURNS TO KYOTO. I AM ALONE AT NIGHT, BUT AS I SLEPT DURING THE DAY, I AM UNABLE TO FIND SLEEP. I SEARCH FOR THE NOTES I HAD WRITTEN AT THE UNREAL DWELLING AND RECOPY THEM.

That night, so many years ago, it was a quarter moon. Near the mountains, the sky was yellow, and green right above, then blended into a deep blue. A few clouds still illuminated by the sun, outlined in pink and charcoal. On that night, so many years ago, that night of another life, of another universe, of another way of walking.

It was not a problem then to tread the ground. Celina's bones were firm and solid, a meticulously organized skeletal structure, inside her body. They were a miracle, her bones. And it was a miracle the flesh and skin covering her bones. Her skin still twitched with her memories of the sense of touch.

She could hear Marco playing with Alice in the living room. They were playing chess. The father was teaching some opening that would later serve as ammunition for the occasional arrogance of the daughter in the presence of adults.

She could imagine her, Alice, sitting up straight and serious, thin, her long hair that had been even longer a few weeks earlier but there had been that apparently incurable lice epidemic at school and the solution was to cut it, once again. Her saucy hair, with so many waves, eternally tangled, which Alice did not take care of in the least.

She could imagine her frowning with her chin resting on her hands, lying on the living room floor, in her yellow shorts and her knit shirt, the faint odor of perspiration because she had spent the afternoon riding her bicycle with her friend. While Marco and Celina. And the memory of the T-shirt binding Celina's hands, and what Marco would do if it were their last day. And the deafening bliss of the last day, which he knew how to delay in her until even the air was writhing around her. Only Marco. Only Marco knew, only Marco could perpetuate that supreme audacity of knowing who Celina was, of knowing what Celina was.

That night, so many years before, the voices of Marco and Alice in the living room, sporadic and friendly.

In the dark room, Celina looked at the ever-darkening sky through the window, and was reminded of a poem that spoke of crow blue, this color that now seemed to absorb the sky of the last day in velvet. The apocalypse dispensing with the horsemen, without any biblical grandeur whatsoever.

A sky of death sealed by the deafening afternoon bliss. And the moon hanging there inertly with its false brilliance, star of mistakes. Beautiful, the moon, so beautiful.

Haruki

One day, on the Rio de Janeiro subway, a woman asked him, as Haruki got off at Botafogo Station: Excuse me, but I was just so curious. Was that book you were reading in Japanese or Chinese? He got off at Shibuya Station and had to hold his breath. It was sprinkling in the Tokyo early evening. There were hordes of umbrellas around him. The noise was alarming, yes, high heels popping on the sidewalks, whistles at traffic lights, voices, gigantic lighted billboards dispersing music and more voices, and somewhere, more voices approaching, in front of a restaurant, irasshaimase—welcome!—in front of a store, irasshaimase, televisions and video games, irasshaimase, but in some place, Haruki heard the fundamental silence. As densely populated as that space might be, Haruki could glimpse the abysm between one atom and another, and the silent void between one sound and another.

It is a fact that the world is more nonexistent than existent. The world is less. Even though it may be filled with feats, facts, words, sounds, images, constructions, umbrellas, a bookstore like the one I am entering and leaping up the escalators to reach the top floor—how many are there? Ten, did I count right?—even without understanding the covers of the books and magazines, these ten floors of books, let's say that there are ten, can collapse at any moment at my feet, because within them there is much more space, much more silence. Many more nonwords than words.

It was neither astonishment nor amazement. Haruki in fact was not even searching for the word that would give meaning to that early evening in Tokyo.

He was possibly searching for the something that would give meaning to the fact that he was there: Yukiko's hands.

Or Celina's hands, which had stayed behind in Kyoto?

Hands, the gesture of holding hands, of sharing. To share Tokyo with someone, the old city of Edo, the Edo of Matsuo Bashō, three hundred—more than three hundred—years later.

But hands—what were they? A genuine support? Could they forge paths among the voices? Could they safely navigate among the immense invisible spaces of Tokyo, the abysms of Tokyo, which the more vertical it became and the more it provoked the illusion of denseness, the more it exploded in infinities?

But what were those very hands, Yukiko's, so familiar and so distant, and Celina's, so close and so unfamiliar, and what would those hands be, if linked to Haruki's own hands, if not a mere thought?

My hands are the size of Tokyo. Tokyo fits into my hands.

Haruki had read it somewhere: scientists have discovered that the same areas of the brain are activated when you see an object and when you remember that object with your eyes closed. He closed his eyes and remembered Yukiko's familiar hands and he remembered Celina's unfamiliar hands.

Yukiko had small hands and thin fingers. But they were strong, her hands. When she typed on the computer keyboard, she made a considerable amount of noise. Haruki had had the opportunity to verify that more than once.

Celina had hands that seemed barely to exist. Wing like hands. Haruki had never touched her hands. Perhaps they would disintegrate upon being touched.

Latino music somewhere, going past his ears. Hombre pequeñito, was what he thought he heard. Hombre. Pequeñito. Little man, ordinary man. I am an ordinary man, like anyone, deceived between pain and pleasure—it had been a while since he had heard that song, years ago he had had it on a Caetano Veloso LP, that is to say, not the LP, but a cassette tape that he had recorded of someone else's LP. I will live and die like an ordinary man.

"Peter Gast." Haruki took the elevator up to the Thai restaurant. He had a note in his pocket. An address. Someone he should look up. A couple, friends of his publishers, who were living in Tokyo, studying.

Haruki was early. He sat down and ordered a beer. A silent toast to his deceased father. To your health, old man, wherever you may be. What would you think of Tokyo? When were you here for the last time? Was it forty, fifty years ago? Could it be that you would recognize Tokyo?

And why did we never talk of these things? And why did I never pay any attention to you, you now regrettably absent old man, when you wanted to talk to me about these things? And why did I never care about your (my) Japanese origins, and why did I never think my eyes were any more slanted than any other Brazilian's? Why was it that I ignored you, and myself as well?

Why was it that one day I ended up with a Japanese descendant as a lover? Would you have approved? A lover, in the first place. The type of lover like Yukiko, in the second place. My little Yukiko who was never mine—can it be that her hands in my brain's memory, those hands that type so heavily, are as real as the hands that I actually saw and touched?

Yukiko and her hands. We were together only a few times. Too few times. For too long a period. Almost always in the afternoon. The first afternoon I used my hands to take off Yukiko's clothes as if I were fulfilling a sacred ritual. With reverence, was the word she used, afterwards, to describe—to describe me.

The first afternoon she passed her hand inside my mouth. She touched my tongue with the tip of her finger. With the tips of two fingers. I closed my mouth around the tips of Yukiko's fingers. She closed her eyes and groaned, which is when everything began to become irreparable.

Slowly, and with both hands, I searched out the place where her hair started to grow, at the nape of her neck. A microcosmos. The skin invaded by the fuzz of her hair.

Too delicate for me to bear. Love bordering on anger. Things like that should die before coming into the world, they should remain suspended in some parallel reality, things like that should recognize, before they materialize, that matter is not their terrain, not their genre, and that they should restrict themselves to unadulterated dreams, to daydreams. To imagination. Things like that should leave the world alone.

Haruki took a brochure out of his backpack.

Welcome to Tokyo—Handy Guide.

Tokyo Metropolitan Government.

SHIBUYA—HARAJUKU—OMOTESANDŌ

On the cover of the brochure, a woodcut done by Utamaro Kitagawa. Ukiyo-e, courtesy of the National Museum of Tokyo.

Eighteenth Century. Ukiyo-e, says the note: images of a floating world.

General Information for Tourists.

Spring (from March to May) and autumn (from September to November) are quite pleasant. Tokyo has relatively mild winters, whereas summers are hot and humid. June and September experience more rainfall than the other months.

The currency is the yen (¥).

There is a 5 percent sales tax. Tourists from abroad can make tax-free purchases in certain department stores by showing their passports.

Voltage: 100 V AC.

Frequency: 60 Hz in western Japan and 50 Hz in eastern Japan.

Haruki took another sip of beer. The couple, his publisher's friends, would soon arrive.

At the table next to him a boy folded a square piece of blue paper. Haruki watched the folds. From the sheet of paper there emerged a bird, a crane, tsuru, its wings spread wide and its tail erect. Its small neck held up straight.

Walking Around Tokyo.

· Daily subway pass: Unlimited rides on any Tokyo subway line for the entire day from the first to the last train. It can be bought in advance or on the day to be used.

Taxi: Raise your hand, stop a taxi, enter the car and tell the driver where you want to go.

JUNE 23RD

I bought some origami paper today, earlier. I had never been interested in origami. I bought a small package with some sheets and there were instructions included to make a tsuru, a crane. I chose a blue sheet and carefully began to join the points.

At a certain moment I realized that the final result, the bird, was not important. What was truly enjoyable was joining the points together and the effort involved in folding. Perhaps I would never attain the tsuru, as simple as those folds might be. When I reached the end, something might be lost.

Unless.

With this thought in mind, I completed the bird. Its wings spread wide and its tail erect. Its small neck held up straight.

I left the apartment. At the entrance to the library there were some vases with flowers, I had already noticed them. I went over with my small tsuru, my small origami debut. I placed the tsuru in one of the flower vases, there were yellow flowers, the paper bird turned bluer in contrast. The beak was slightly blunt. I hope no Japanese saw me doing that. The clumsy, awkward Western girl.

22nd day

RAIN IN THE MORNING. NO VISITORS, AND IN MY SOLITUDE I AMUSE MYSELF BY WRITING RANDOMLY, INCLUDING THE FOLLOWING:

HE WHO MOURNS MAKES GRIEF HIS MASTER; HE WHO DRINKS MAKES PLEASURE HIS MASTER. WHEN SAIGYŌ WROTE "WERE IT NOT FOR SOLITUDE, SADNESS WOULD DESTROY ME," HE MADE SOLITUDE HIS MASTER. IN ANOTHER POEM HE WROTE:

> IN THE MOUNTAIN VILLAGE
> TO WHOM CALLS
> THE SMALL CUCKOO?
> I CAME HERE DETERMINED
> TO LIVE ALL ALONE.

yamazato ni
ko wa mata tare o
yobukodori
hitori sumamu to
omoishi mono o

THERE IS NOTHING IS MORE PLEASURABLE THAN SOLITUDE.
THE HERMIT CHŌSHŌ WROTE: "IF A GUEST FINDS PEACE FOR
HALF A DAY, THE HOST LOSES IT FOR HALF A DAY." SODŌ LIKES
TO REPEAT THOSE WORDS. I DO AS WELL; BY THE WAY, FINDING
MYSELF ALONE IN A MONASTERY, I COMPOSED THESE LINES:

FILLED WITH GRIEF
BRING ME LONELINESS—
MOUNTAIN CUCKOO

uki ware o
sabishigarase yo
kankodori

AS EVENING FALLS THEY BRING ME A MESSAGE FROM KYORAI.
HE TELLS ME THAT OTOKUNI HAS RETURNED FROM EDO, AND I
RECEIVE MANY MESSAGES FROM FRIENDS AND DISCIPLES.
AMONG OTHERS IS A NOTE FROM KYOKUSUI, SAYING THAT UPON
VISITING MY HUT OF THE BANANA TREE, WHICH I ABANDONED,
THERE HE FOUND SŌHA.

SO LONG AGO
WHO WASHED THE LITTLE POTS?
VIOLETS IN BLOOM

mukashi tare
konabe araishi

sumiregusa

(Sōha)

HE ALSO WRITES: "WHERE I NOW LIVE, THERE IS NO GREEN
WHATSOEVER WITH THE EXCEPTION OF A MAPLE TREE THE
HEIGHT OF TWO BOWS."

THE YOUNG MAPLE
TURNS TO BROWN
IN A FLOURISH

waka kaede
chairo ni naru mo
hito sakari
(Sōha)

IN RANSETSU'S LETTER:

BEHOLD
AMIDST THE DUST OF SHOOTS
FERNS ARE THE CHOSEN

zenmai no
chiri ni eraruru
warabi kana

SERVANTS' DAY OF REST
IN THE CHILDREN'S HEARTS
MELANCHOLY

degawari ya
osanagokoro
mono aware

IN THE OTHER LETTERS THERE ARE NUMEROUS MOVING OR
POIGNANT TALES.

Celina and Marco

The things that reminded her of Marco.

Two beer coasters: Alchemy Ale, Pints Pub, Denver, Colorado. Notations scribbled on his huge Greenpeace calendar that used to hang in the kitchen (numbers that only he knew the meaning of, initials, words abbreviated in some sort of personal shorthand). A stuffed furry blue seal. A postcard someone had sent from Germany.

A box of photographs from the time of his adolescence, when he was into photography and had a laboratory set up in the maid's room at his father's house. The guitar that he no longer played, but had to have on hand because you never know.

The Ming Aralia, *a árvore da felicidade*, the tree of happiness.

The drawer where he kept, in peaceful confusion, paper clips, business cards picked up here and there, social security booklets, a broken stapler, check stubs, marijuana in a small can, his favorite cigarette paper (Ledinha, transparent cigarette paper, Brazilian smoke culture. Mini. 100% cellulose—natural— transparent. Does not need glue. Non-plastic biodegradable sheets. Attention: Store in a cool, dry place. Ministry of Health Warning: Smoking is bad for your health. Prohibited for minors under 18).

The things that Marco had told Celina that she remembered once in a while. A mountaineering ex-girlfriend with a T-shirt that said: Girls like to climb on top. The day that he tied the dog's mouth up with a rubber band and then the dog bit him. His first car that got nine miles to the gallon. The night that he saw Saturn through the telescope and Saturn was a white, brilliant dot surrounded by a white, brilliant ring. The Chinese sword from the time that he took tai chi lessons. The petting session on a bus trip to Argentina with a girl who was a stranger (and afterward they both stood up and he realized that the girl was very, but very much taller than he) when he was nineteen.

The things that Celina no longer knew which of them had bought, whether it was her or Marco or the two of them together. The Keith Jarrett CD, the Cologne concert. The blue wine opener. The green lamp from Lavradio Street. The huge transparent glass vase where they kept their wine cork collection. The nail clippers. The Chagall poster that hung in the bathroom. The incense holder. The ceramic pots from Monte Sião.

The things that Celina no longer knew which of them had lost, whether it was her or Marco or the two of them together. The Edward Lear book. He said she had lent it to someone and forgotten about it. The orange umbrella. She said he had forgotten it on the bus. The refrigerator magnet from the Toy Museum in Sintra—someone had brought it back from a trip. The Spanish-Portuguese dictionary. The first tooth that Alice lost (the lower left central incisor, as Marco had learned and memorized, but that did not prevent the tooth from disappearing) and that was kept, according to witnesses, in a certain envelope, in a certain box, in a certain drawer. The remote control for the TV.

First, Celina and Marco lived in an apartment in the Catete neighborhood where they barely had space for a double bed. It was on the top floor, close to the elevator machinery. The machinery crackled and hummed, it gave noisy jolts. Luckily, the building was small, five floors, ten apartments, so the manifestations of the elevator were actually sporadic. It was out of the question to try and install a crib for their daughter: something would have to go. The refrigerator, the oven, the table. Celina bought a baby buggy and Alice, so tiny, slept there, with so much empty space around her that she looked more like an empress in a king-sized bed.

The Catete apartment was close to the bakery, the supermarket, the health clinic where Alice took those vaccines that would give her fever for two days, the secondhand store that sold rare LPs, the Museum of the Republic, the day nursery where Celina and Marco enrolled Alice when she turned four months old, so that they would be able to, basically, sleep and work, in that order.

On weekends Marco took her for outings in the museum's gardens. When she dozed off, in her buggy, he would sit near the ice-cream cart and read his newspaper and ask for a chocolate ice-cream bar. Women of all ages, from fifteen to eighty, would glance at him with tender expressions and eloquent smiles: how lovely, a father taking care of his small baby. They thought it to be an essentially female task, and there was a relative degree of masculine concession in that beautiful portrait of man and baby.

Her father. The strength with which Alice would close her hand around Marco's little finger suggested that in her most secret consciousness she perhaps knew everything. Or that she was just instinctively being an infant, like so many before and after her. Her legs curled up, her arms curled. Her skull bones still not joined and her brain lightly pulsating through the cracks—it shocked Marco to learn this, that the human being was fragile to that point. Her neck so weak you could barely believe there was a vertebral column passing through inside. Her umbilical cord hanging like a noodle that someone had forgotten in the refrigerator for six months.

What it was like to love someone forever.

One night, years later, Celina and Alice were looking at the sky. Near the flowing river. Up high in the sky, Celina pointed out Fomalhaut, the brightest star in Piscis Austrinus.

It's close to here. A star that is actually two stars.

I can only see one.

They're very close to one another. They're separated by one light-year. That means if you were on one of the Fomalhaut stars and traveled to the sister star—You already explained it to me, the I-don't-know-how-many miles per second—186 thousand, it would take a year.

And from here to there?

Twenty-three. There below, follow the tip of my finger, there, do you see? It looks like a cloud. It's a galaxy. It's much farther away. It would take you thirty thousand years to get there. At the speed of light.

Why do you know these things?

Because I do.

Alice laughed. Oh, my. She wrapped her thin arms around Celina's arm. Alice was all clavicles and tibias and kneecaps.

They both stood there, alone with the Fomalhaut sisters and a few billion other stars, many already dead, separated from them by magic distances.

What would it be like to have the object of your research residing thirty thousand light-years away? Without amphora fragments to help you, or apocryphal manuscripts, or fossilized skeletons of gigantic reptiles? Just you, and the past, and the distances?

Once Celina had read a quotation from *Essays in Idleness* by Yoshida Kenkō: Pleasure does not only come from looking at the moon and the flowers with our own eyes. To do nothing more than think of those things, on a spring day, even if we stay at home, or on a moonlit night, even if we don't leave our alcove, offers us joy and delight.

The forms of happiness. On the banks of the river listening to the water bearing the spirits down from the mountains. The completely overcast sky. Observing intently, it was possible to see the entire river, organic, a fluid serpent between the stones.

Sharpening your ears, it was possible to hear the river breathing. The river traveling.

The forms of happiness. The completely overcast sky and it began to rain on the banks of the river. And the two of them, Marco and Celina, trapped beneath a small roof that began to truly be small because the rain fell harder and now it was rain with wind and the spirits that the river bore were now made of mud.

Beautiful clay spirits submerged in the water.

The forms of happiness. A frog. A pair of earrings.

The forms of happiness.

Orange-flavored lip gloss. On her tongue.

The forms of happiness. The cicadas that abandoned their old, hollow skeletons on tree trunks. Coffee.

The forms of happiness. Childrens' drawings stuck on the wall. He said: Stay right here: right here, Doing Nothing.

While he read (a sneeze), he would caress his left wrist, the wrist that held the book. What exactly did the word "indulgence" mean?

Children coming home from school, along the road. The dark-skinned children. At high noon, the November sun. The forms of happiness. The river, the flowing river, where he dove in, the icy water that made his skin icy as well.

Sex in the afternoon, as if afternoons were made specifically for that purpose. The afternoons for sex. As if you shouldn't do anything else. As if not. Icy bodies out of the water. Nipples on icy breasts. Warm recesses between two legs.

The forms of happiness.

Flowing between the stones on the perpetual voyage of the river. And the spirits coming from afar. And the river.

Once a small amount of water fell onto an oily surface. Rainbows began to wiggle like tiny, agitated worms. Once the water in the teapot began to boil, and the bubbles burst their instantaneous lives and the steam rose to the ceiling in its humid death. Once Alice was scolded and punished and when Marco went into her room, moments later, she had fallen asleep on the made-up bed, on top of the yellow dog-print bedspread, an open-eyed dog, a closed-eyed girl. Once Marco had heard Alice's heart beating in Celina's belly, amplified by the doctor's machines. He had the feeling that the whole world had a basic, essential, primordial rhythm.

To have severed all the links, the ties, everything that led to him. Except for the heartache. Celina dropped down to 105 pounds. Around her eyes, two black circles of resistance, a fierce resistance to what she knew not.

She wandered about the house. The mountain pointed its gigantic tooth up to the sky, not a lower central incisor, but a canine tooth, painful, misplaced, made of black stone.

Her feet would guide Celina, her brittle body, as if on a long trip from the living room to the bedroom to the bathroom to the living room to the veranda door that framed the tremendous stone canine tooth.

On her first day without medication she felt a sort of permanent punch to the stomach, a punch from the inside out. Her stomach, wanting to spit itself out into a corner of two walls and stay there, dead, returned to normalcy. Her incompetent stomach unable to digest food—but Celina knew that her weight had only changed places, migrated from other parts of the body to her stomach. Everything concentrating there, dense and compact, to the point of not creating any volume.

It wasn't a weight of bones, muscles, viscera, fat. It was a weight of weight in itself. Of essence. The scales might say 105 pounds: the scales understood nothing of weight. There within her stomach were at least so many more, multiplied by ten, by one hundred.

There was the loneliness of a glass of water. And her feet insisting, the body insisting with her feet throughout the house.

They told her that time would go by. They guaranteed her so. Take her feet throughout the house, or trust them, her own feet, perhaps that might help turn the clock on that first day, the first day without medication.

A silence of the dead on the fields of battle. A hue of dried blood. Amputated arms. Blank eyes. On these occasions everything changes. All the proportions. All the clocks. All the words.

The first day without medication was a day that the Flamengo and Vasco soccer teams played at Maracanã Stadium. Celina heard the voices coming from the street. A mystery. Voices, yells, firecrackers. The noise from the firecrackers at least made sense.

On these occasions you don't know how dawn will break. What color the sky will be. On these occasions, you don't know if dawn will break. An exercise in resistance—that Celina knew. How is it that these troops of resistance organize themselves, and how they survive, against all odds.

Haruki and Bashō

In the early hours of one particular morning, his blunt pencil drew her ankle and its small protruding bone. Yukiko did not move. She was asleep. Light began to filter into the room through the cracks in the window. The illustrator knew that he would be unable to sleep. He needed to finish his sketch, before dawn broke.

The sleeping woman's body was almost phosphorescent. Fatuous fire. A vein throbbed in her neck and her back undulated rhythmically, ever so slowly, with her respiration.

It had to be you, he said, out loud. It is as if you weren't alive, no matter how much I watch that vein throb in your neck.

He imagined the warm air that she was exhaling. He imagined that behind her eyes she was dreaming she was a butterfly.

The sleeping woman was dreaming that a man was sketching her ankle with its small protruding bone. In her dream, she moved. Her eyes and her arms were open.

Haruki stopped sketching. The artist who now no longer drew made an invitation and a promise to her. But he didn't say anything. It was simply a gesture, simply a way of interrupting his sketching and looking up, and a thread stretched from his eyes to hers. A bridge made of spider silk.

In her memory, her father's voice said: We can only see a spider web due to the reflection of the sunlight. The diameter of its thread is too small to be seen by the human eye. Hito no me ni chiisasugimasu. Too small to be seen by the human eye.

In Tokyo, Haruki walked through Fukagawa, where centuries before the Banana Hut, Bashōan, could be found.

The small cottage was built on the banks of the Sumida River. The city was called Edo, centuries earlier. Much later it would change names, as the poets also changed their names, and it began to be known as Tokyo. In Edo lived the shogun, the military leader, and it was from there that he controlled Japan, in spite of the fact that His Imperial Majesty ruled in Kyoto, the capital. Between one city and the other, the Tōkaidō, the road that carried merchants, samurai companies, and pilgrims.

Haruki thinks: unbeknownst to the poet, a mosquito poised on Matsuo Bashō's hand sucks his blood. On the simple altar, a small image of the Buddha, carved in wood, is enveloped in delicate shadows as day breaks—his legs in the lotus position, his thin torso with one of his shoulders exposed, the right hand on his knee and the left in his lap, the cupped palm turned upward. His long earlobes, his half-open eyes. A faint smile on his lips. The lotus flower petals upon which he is seated begin to glow vaguely, anticipating the first hint of sunlight inside the cottage. The ashes of incense burned the evening before lie scattered in front of the statue, in a random trail. The banana tree outside gently stirs.

Asleep, Bashō flutters his hand, to free himself of the nuisance. The mosquito goes to hide in the shadows, behind the image of the Buddha, who will without doubt protect it.

The travels of Bashō. Who once wrote:

TRAVELER —

THAT IS MY NAME

THE FIRST RAIN OF WINTER

The journey is always for the journey in itself. It is to have the road once more beneath your feet. Bashō's home, like that of the navigators, like that of those men who spend their lives herding cattle, is anywhere. It is where the journey decides to take them.

Many people died on the road. Among them, the poets Du Fu, Li Bai, Saigyō, and Sōgi. Like clouds dissipating in the sky. The months and the days are nothing more than pilgrims. Thus said the Chinese poet Li Bai, centuries earlier: the sky and the earth and all of the cosmos are in the sphere of transformation. Light and darkness, the sun and the moon are, in the same way, eternal travelers. The floating world is nothing more than a dream, and all human pleasures are ephemeral.

When Bashō died, the Bashōan was preserved as a historical site on a samurai's property, said the informative pamphlet that Haruki had picked up. But it disappeared sometime at the end of the nineteenth century. After the 1917 flood, they discovered a stone frog there, of which, it was said, Bashō had been very fond. Shortly thereafter, the Tokyo government designated that address, Tokiwa 1-3, the historical site of Bashōan.

A small sanctuary in the garden. Over the wall, Haruki could see the river, the Sumida, the wide Sumida River, so different from the river that saw Bashō and which was seen by Bashō, and so very much the same.

The river, its invisible stones, the traveling river.

Too small to be seen by the human eye. Yukiko lasted a year in Haruki's life. They had known one another for some time. They knew one another professionally through some publisher, and they began to know one another less bureaucratically with the passage of the weeks and the months until one day Haruki sketched her for the first time. Nude.

He only came to truly know her after the sketch. It was the sketch that drew her closer, but coming closer Yukiko drew away at the same time, she had her life that pulled her to the surface like a buoy, and her dive, at some moment, would invariably undergo a backspin and turn into a drowning. A wave that crashed and receded. A sea stretching forward and pulling back once again. It was imperative to swim back, to take a breath.

She had to burst up through the water once more, to invert the plunge, to escape. Discourage being startled. Restore the status quo. Basically that was it.

Yukiko and her life. Yukiko—too small to be seen by the human eye, a thread of spider web that blinded Haruki when, for an instant, he saw the sun hit it. And it sparkled. The girl with slanted eyes, like his own. Nisei—second generation. The daughter of Japanese immigrants.

Unlike Haruki, extremely knowledgeable about Japan. Unlike Haruki, fluent in Japanese. A translator of Japanese. Among other things. She had studied at a university in Tokyo.

Only once had Haruki and Yukiko traveled together. For two days. There was a beach on that trip. There was laughter as well, instants squeezed within the closed fist of their secret. Two days that didn't exist in the official version. A different padding, very distinct from those that pad the Fontainebleau Treaties and the Elba Islands of history.

On that trip, there were ripe cashew fruits and cachaça, sugar-cane brandy. They both laughed themselves silly at the peanuts that had fallen on the ground. There was that AND IF hanging in the air like a mobile, like a wind chime, rattling the entire time, beckoning—AND IF, AND IF, AND IF. Sounding metallic and soft, as well it should.

On Sunday they returned to Rio de Janeiro and to their houses and to their other respective masks. The traffic on the highway was ugly and gray, and the city was wrapped in a crust of pollution.

Yukiko was so small, too small to be seen by the human eye. But he felt compelled to draw her, insistently, religiously.

JUNE 24TH

The journey is always for the journey in itself. It is to have the road once more beneath your feet. There is always an AND IF somewhere.

AND IF I hadn't come to Kyoto with Haruki,

AND IF Haruki and I had entered different cars on the subway,

AND IF it hadn't been raining that afternoon,

AND IF I hadn't seen the book in his hands,

AND IF he and I had decided it would be sex from the beginning, or at least it would be sex at some point before this moment in which I write, now,

AND IF I weren't writing, now,

AND IF Alice didn't particularly like riding a bicycle,

AND IF Marco hadn't tied my hands to the headboard with the red T-shirt that I was wearing,

AND IF I had been born an hour later,

AND IF Marco or Alice or Haruki or Bashō or Bashō's translator (her name is Yukiko Sakade) had been born an hour later.

Haruki told me that he knows the translator of this diary by Bashō. He told me reluctantly. As if he couldn't find the right words.

She must be the woman he loves.

AND IF Yukiko is the woman Haruki loves.

AND IF Yukiko had come to Japan with Haruki.

Yukiko Sakade—not I. Not Celina.

AND IF this journey were a different journey.

23rd day

I CLAP MY HANDS

THE ECHO ANSWERS, AT DAWN

SUMMER MOON

> *te o uteba*
>
> *kodama ni akuru*
>
> *natsu no tsuki*

BAMBOO SHOOTS

THE CHILDHOOD DRAWINGS

I LOVED TO DO

> *take no ko ya*
>
> *osanaki toki no*
>
> *e no susami*

DAY AFTER DAY

THE BARLEY RIPENS

SKYLARKS SING

hitohi hitohi
mugi akaramite
naku hibari

I HAVE NO TALENT

AND I ONLY WISH TO SLEEP

BIRDS SING LOUDLY

nō nashi no
nemutashi ware o
gyōgyōshi

Celina and Marco

The journey is always for the journey in itself. It is to have the road once more beneath your feet. Haruki copied the phrase and sent it by e-mail to Celina. From a cybercafé in Tokyo to the computer that the research center in Kyoto had lent him.

Celina put water on to boil. To make some coffee with heaps of coffee grounds. The coffee she had bought tasted like barley. No problem. She could solve that by using lots of coffee.

She sat on the veranda, picked up some papers to read and forgot that the water was boiling. When she remembered, the bubbles were bursting in desperation, hampering one another, completely and totally dazed, stunned.

Celina picked up the teapot handle without first testing the temperature. She held it firmly and lifted it off the burner. It was very hot. Too hot. With an involuntary gesture she released the teapot, which fell. The boiling water spread out in a rapid wave. It immediately became a dark stain on the floor. With her hand aching from the burn, Celina retrieved two ice cubes from the freezer, held them, and then her pain was mixed in with the cold, and the cold made her forget her pain.

JUNE 24TH *(After My Burn)*

Pain. An undesirable truth in a world of analgesics. Never, pain. Never feel it quiet and hot in the middle of your body, never let it shiver in your hands or break out in a cold sweat on your forehead, never let pain hurt.

Here's the big catch. My pain is mine: the mark on my skin, made bright red by the burn. It exists like a visitor in the living room. Pain, a little old lady seated in the corner of the sofa.

That was, perhaps, what most disrupted relationships with the world: the generalized prejudice against pain. Thus there were so many pills of every shape and size, bottles of alcohol and other legal drugs, illegal drugs, every sort of narcotic. So many armchairs in front of televisions on Sunday nights, while a show of insanities glides across the screen. So many disguises. Deep down, all of these things with the same disguised objective: so pain wouldn't hurt. So pain would just shut up, shrink up, surrender, muzzle itself, be tamed.

In Kyoto, entirely alone, Celina felt her right hand ache. She observed the smooth skin of her burn. She felt the surface with the tips of her left fingers. Why not. She blew on the spot. Her hot breath increased the pain. Why not. Why not just give in to what hurts, to what is undesirable, ugly, absurd, ridiculous.

Six years earlier, pain had appeared in her life like a monster leaping out of the closet. The alligator hidden under the bed that could bite her hand, if she left it hanging outside of the covers.

It arrived with questions in tow.

But why had everything been so comfortable until then?

But why the sunshine, bliss, smiles? The flowing river, the wind?

But why the fullness of quiet hours, if within the pads of their fingers those hours contained needles?

Then the quiet revolution of her steps took place. The little old lady seated on the sofa gave notice that she was not leaving. She asked for a cup of coffee, a tea, a glass of water. Celina decided to serve her. And she perceived that this sufficed: to be careful of the steps she took. If they touched the right places, everything else would be all right. She walked through her living room with her visitor observing her. She placed one foot in front of the other in front of the other in front of the other. She served the coffee, the tea, the glass of water.

On her computer, the e-mail message Haruki had sent from Tokyo glowed brightly on the screen. The journey is always for the journey in itself. It is to have the road once more beneath your feet.

With the painful fingers of her right hand Celina held the mouse. She moved the cursor. She clicked Reply.

Six years earlier, on that afternoon in which her cell phone rang differently, Celina was walking down Presidente Vargas Avenue.

She was coming from DETRAN, Brazil's Department of National Transportation. Inside, in the tepid bubble of bureaucratic tedium, huge silver fans moved through the air that despite the agitation remained static. Even the wind was still in there. It was a timeless place. Things neither happened nor ceased to happen. People on their pilgrimages resigned themselves, and even those who were not resigned were resignedly unresigned.

An upset middle-class woman said: That's Brazil for you. They looked at her as if she were from outer space. A vendor walked about selling chocolates and chewing gum. The staircase was sad looking and the walls were inexpressive. The noise was inexpressive, no matter how intense it might be.

Behind the receptionists there was a huge sign. Disrespectful conduct directed toward a civil servant by reason of the performance of his or her duty: a crime punishable by detention from 6 (six) months to 2 (two) years, or by fine (Article 331 of the Penal Code).

And it was all so gigantically, contagiously tiresome.

But outside, in compensation, the world recovered all at once. The street vendors cried out colors, textures, shapes, trinkets. One had a handwritten poster that said here the devil doesn't dare come in, and if he does he runs right out. There was incense for sale and funk music in the background. Walking in front of her was a young black man, sweating heavily, and on the back of his T-shirt was written Surfing is life, the rest is details. He was swinging a white plastic bag, and Celina could hear the noise, the crackling of the plastic.

Celina carried papers in her purse. A wonderful book that she was enjoying reading. She was headed toward the subway station. Then her cell phone rang inside her purse, and it was a ring capable of knocking the earth off of its axis for a second.

It was the same ring as always. A simple, telephone-like ring. None of those emulations of Mozart symphonies. And, nevertheless, it was not the same, it would never again be the same, never again the noise, the DETRAN fans, the Presidente Vargas street vendors, the chocolates and chewing gum, Article 331 of the Penal Code, the funk, the devil, the surfing and the details, never again could these things sprout from the earth's surface with the same spontaneity.

Haruki, she typed. I was thinking about the translator of *Saga nikki.* I was curious to know more about her. If you feel like telling me, of course.

June 25th

E-mail. You write something, click on a button and that's it. Why did I go and mention the Bashō translator to Haruki. What business of mine is that. What kind of intimacy do I have with him. As if I could actually say that we were friends. As if I could be certain that we had constructed that. We ran into each other in the middle of a mountain of AND IFs. We came to Japan together, which is nothing more than another AND IF, nothing more than a card from the deck, among so many others that we could have chosen or have let someone choose for us.

I spent the afternoon in the research center's library. I entered into the middle of those mobile metallic corridors, that are created and destroyed at the touch of a red button, and I randomly ran my eyes across the book spines.

I found *Makura no sōshi,* by the Japanese writer Sei Shō-nagon—*The Pillow Book,* in an English translation.

Sei Shōnagon and her lists: Things that cannot be compared (summer and winter; night and day; rain and sunshine). Depressing things (a dog howling during the day). Hateful things. Rare things (avoiding ink stains in the notebook where we copy stories, poems, or things of that sort). Things that are nearby though they be far away. Things that lose something when painted (cherry blossoms, yellow roses). Things that gain something when painted (a very cold winter scene, an unbearably hot summer scene).

Different ways of talking: The speech of a priest. The speech of men and of women. Simple folk tend to add extra syllables to their speech.

Sei Shōnagon wrote *The Pillow Book* in the eleventh century. I brought it back with me. It's here next to me, open, right next to the loose pages of the translation that Yukiko Sakade did of *Saga Diary*.

I see close to me the zori I bought for Alice. The television is turned on and the advertisements in Japanese are totally strange and totally familiar.

I like this familiarity with strangeness, something I suddenly realize. I like feeling somewhat apart, someone who doesn't belong, who doesn't understand, who doesn't speak. To occupy a space that doesn't seem to exist. As if I weren't made of flesh and blood, but were merely, merely a dream, as if I were made of flowers and papers and an origami tsuru and the echo of the leap of a frog inside an old pond or the echo of the high heels of a woman walking down the sidewalk and the evocations of Sei Shōnagon and of Bashō, centuries later.

What is the place that I occupy in the world? Does it have a name, this place? Does it have dimensions? Height, width, depth? Could it be nothing more than a sound, or a gesture, or an odor, or an unexplored possibility? The opposite of sound? The opposite of a gesture—immobility, potentiality. Giving up?

I have no idea why, but I am thinking about Marco now and about a conversation we once had.

We were sitting at the table. It was at night and it was hot. I can remember my elbows resting on the wood, forming an upside-down V with the angle at the tip of my chin, where my hands were joined together. Leftover food and drinks scattered about.

Marco looked into my eyes; he looked at me like someone who had an important and difficult message to deliver. And then he said to me: You are so beautiful.

That luminous sentence. In that explosion of happiness something clicked, and I said: I noticed something.

What, he asked.

The words cute, beautiful, and pretty have totally different meanings. When you say to me you are so cute, when you call me pretty, and when you say you are so beautiful. Those are totally different things.

Marco smiled.

When I say pretty, he said, I think I mean something physical, you know? When I say cute, it's because of something endearing you've said or done. But when you're beautiful it's because the inside and the outside have come together.

I don't know why I thought of that now. I don't know why I remember the song that was playing: "when I die bury me in Lapinha." We were listening to it turned way up to drown out the neighbor's loud music without being terribly mindful of the fact that if the entire world followed that line of logic our planet would be a single scream of horror, out of tune with itself. A land of perforated eardrums.

I turn off the television. On doing that, I don't know what the sentence that I interrupted in the middle meant. I don't know what the next expression was on the face that I interrupted, I only know that it is 11 P.M. here and 11 A.M. in the country I come from and that the consistency of all this is so precarious that it takes a burden off of my shoulders and allows me to go to bed.

One day Marco and Celina had a conversation. They were sitting at the table. It was at night and it was hot. Celina had her elbows resting on the wood, forming an upside-down V with the angle at the tip of her chin where her hands were joined together. Leftover food and drinks scattered about. Marco looked into her eyes and said: You are so beautiful.

That luminous sentence.

And thirty seconds went by. And three months, and three years went by. And that many more. And the slivers of that luminous sentence flew into the air, determined to turn into something else, since nothing, absolutely nothing, is lost, since everything begets everything else.

Yukiko and Bashō

JUNE 26TH

Haruki answered the e-mail message I sent him with reservations. He wrote: Yukiko has been an acquaintance of mine for several years. We haven't seen each other lately. Her parents are Japanese. She also lives in Rio, but far away from me. It was she who suggested to the publisher that I illustrate Bashō's diary. She once told me something her father had taught her: We can only see a spider web due to the reflection of the sunlight. The diameter of its thread is too small to be seen by the human eye.

Haruki also told me that he would return to Kyoto within two or three days. He still hasn't decided if he will travel farther north. Probably not. He's been checking out prices. But it appears to me that it will be too expensive, he said. The transportation is so expensive in this country!

I think about that woman whose father spoke of spider webs and reflections of sunlight. I imagine her.

I imagine firm hands and short nails. Unpolished nails. Firm hands that type vigorously on the computer keyboard.

A small scar next to her right wrist—a dog bite. When she was a child perhaps she had seen that perfectly sweet cocker spaniel parked in front of the bakery, in a red collar tied to the post, and she had stopped to pet it. It was an old animal, droopy eyelids, glassy eyes. And so it was that Yukiko was bitten by a cocker spaniel.

Thick, dark, straight hair like Haruki's, but hers is long, pulled up on top of her head.

Her back slightly bent over as she types words. Loads of words. Multitudes of words that join the noises of the world. Who knows if she doesn't think: why so many words. Who knows if she doesn't imagine an alternative silence to that Babel.

Perhaps one day, with her back slightly bent over, she was typing words that carried Haruki within them. Perhaps he snuck up on her thoughts from behind, with a kiss and a shiver. A kiss on the nape of her neck, where that baby fuzz of all promises germinates, even those promises that will never be fulfilled. The texture of his tongue on her left earlobe. His hands curving around her shoulders and her breasts. At that moment it is possible that Yukiko stopped typing in the middle of a word.

Des

(Design, desire, despoil, desert, desolation?)

Her two free hands might have moved back to where Haruki, standing, would feel them rubbing against the fabric of his slacks, lightly at first, then pressing with the right amount of pressure, with just the right amount of pressure, nothing more than that. Yukiko's back would now be straight.

Her body would joyfully become moist.

On her right wrist, the small scar from the cocker spaniel bite, the dog that had already long ago become a handful of delicate bones and a faint memory, a memory wandering about alone on the surface of the earth, a ghost of that impulse, an echo of that way it was: a biter. The barely visible scar on Yukiko's right wrist, where other bones and other impulses direct its movement. The fabric of Haruki's slacks, where the movement imprints moments of joy. The body knows how to be happy by itself. The body dispenses with all that silliness regarding souls.

Kyoto continues to not deliver the awaited rains. What had happened to tsuyu, the rainy season, that year? At the research center, in Kyoto, they told Celina that the weather was being kind to the two uninformed Brazilians who had decided to visit Japan during the most unpleasant season of the year.

But at least the name of the season was pleasant. Tsuyu: rainfall of plums, they taught Celina. Because it was during the time of year that plums ripened.

The children made teruteru bōzu, cloth or paper dolls made to summon good weather.

Mister Banana Tree, Matsuo Bashō, Celina read in the introduction that Yukiko Sakade had written for the translation, was born into a family of low-ranking samurai. Samurai: the warriors of feudal Japan.

The Japan that closed itself off from the world for 250 years. The Japan of the Tokugawas, the long dynasty.

In the rainy season without rain, the season of plums ripening and children primed to make magic dolls, Celina read the names of the fourteen shogun, the military chiefs, from the Tokugawa family, who ruled Japan for so long.

Ieyasu. Hidetada. Iemitsu. Ietsuna. Tsunayoshi. Ienobu.

Ietsugu. Yoshimune. Ieshige. Ieharu. Ienari. Ieyoshi. Iesada. Iemochi. And finally the adopted Yoshinobu, the fifteenth shogun.

An absolute state. Ieyasu, the first Tokugawa shogun, established the rules of conduct for the military class, the samurai. As decreed in a document, the samurai should embrace, side by side, the study of literature and the practice of the martial arts. They should denounce any type of scheme that might plot change.

Change: a synonym for revolt.

Private marriages were forbidden. Clothes had to be adequate for the social position and they could not be extravagant. All samurai had to live in a frugal manner.

Tokugawa Ieyasu seized power from the ancient Toyotomi family. He decimated his enemies and displayed their decapitated heads on the road between Fushimi and Kyoto. There were thousands of them. He publicly decapitated the eight-year-old son of Toyotomi Hideyori and a concubine.

Ieyasu rose to glory to the point of becoming deified after his death: Gongen was the title he received. An incarnation of the Buddha.

Bashō, Mister Banana Tree, was born during the government of the third shogun, in 1644, in Iga Province, approximately thirty miles southeast of Kyoto. He first went to serve a young master, Tōdō Yoshitada. Between the two there were strong bonds of friendship and the ties of poetry. They both wrote poetry. They wrote haiku.

When he came of age, he received his samurai name: Matsuo Munefusa. And shortly afterward there was the premature death of Yoshitada, which led Bashō to abandon his home and to adopt a life of wandering.

Wanderer. Traveler. He was twenty-two years old. For convenience's sake? For unresolved love affairs? For a lack of perspectives? For curiosity? He is thought to have gone to Kyoto, where he would have studied poetry, calligraphy, philosophy.

He would later write: at a certain moment in my life it was my ambition to occupy an official position, with the possession of lands. He would also write: there was a time when I was fascinated by homosexual love. And it was never clear who, in his life, was a certain woman who would later become the miko Jutei, a shrine maiden. She might have been mother to a child of Bashō. To more than one child of Bashō.

JUNE 26TH *(At night)*

AND IF, then, this is the woman that Haruki loves,

AND IF true love is the one that abandons its home and adopts a life of wandering,

AND IF this coming to Japan, this job, this book, this poet,

AND IF all of this only serves to put Haruki against the wall, at the razor's edge, beneath the sword, a samurai in a ritual sacrifice? Seppuku, the noble suicide of the samurai: to rip open one's own abdomen, exposing one's entrails, and then to be decapitated by an assistant.

24th day—on the Hut of Fallen Persimmons

GREEN BEAN FIELDS

AND FIREWOOD STOREHOUSES:

BOTH ARE SPECIAL PLACES

mame uuru

hata mo kibeya mo

meisho kana

(BONCHŌ)

AS EVENING FALLS, KYORAI COMES FROM KYOTO.
A LETTER FROM MASAFURU OF ZEZE.
AND ANOTHER FROM SHŌKAKU OF ŌTSU.
BONCHŌ ARRIVES.
THE ABBOT FROM THE HONPUOKU TEMPLE, IN KATADA,
COMES TO VISIT AND SPENDS THE NIGHT. BONCHŌ
RETURNS TO KYOTO.

JUNE 27TH *(Before Dawn)*

I take a small untoward liberty. I search on the internet for the
e-mail address of Haruki's publisher. I send a message. I would
like to get in touch with the translator Yukiko Sakade, with a certain urgency. I appreciate your consideration.

Yukiko's father taught her that we can only see a spider web
due to the reflection of the sunlight. The diameter of its thread is
too small to be seen by the human eye.

Dolls to summon good weather: teruteru bōzu.

I slept for an hour and awoke in the middle of strange dreams.
Dreams not mine. Someone else's imagination. An embrace, but
my body did not feel it, and the arms were unfamiliar. Then my
heart started pounding, and I got up.

Sleep is a necessity: That's what I have learned. That's what so
many people with whom I have come across in life have told me.
But on my own I have discovered that sometimes you need to stay
awake. Hold your eyelids open and hold your breath. This is a
moment of rare acquiescence. My own presence within myself,
without distractions, without the colorful mobiles of my daily
tasks hanging in front of my nose.

An insect comes in from outside, through the open window, to keep me company. It lands on the corner of the table. Its colorful, bright, beautiful body. Its small feet glued to the table, so gently that they barely seem to touch it.

Haruki and Bashō

Alone in Tokyo, Haruki and his publisher's friends had gone to a play that united a company from Indonesia and another from Japan. *Mnemosyne.* From both sides Haruki could hear phrases that accompanied the movements of the beautiful bodies on stage, and from both sides the phrases were hypnotically incomprehensible. For the first time in his life, words did not need meanings, they were simply music, they were a sonorous cultural soup that preceded any genesis.

Afterward he and the couple went to eat Chinese food. Haruki became slightly drunk with the yellow alcohol, the strong Chinese wine, made from rice. Later they said their good-byes and he took the subway to Asakusa Station, the one closest to his hotel. He had found a ryōkan, a traditional hostel, a bit away from the city center. It had a communal *ofuro* with a view of a pagoda.

He was carrying a present for Celina. In one of the bookstores that he had entered he had found that festival of images, haiku and photographs in a thick volume, more than three hundred pages. He opened it, leafed through it. He knew that he would find Bashō at some point, reread or revisited by a photographer almost four hundred years later.

YUKI TO YUKI

KOYOI SHIWASU NO

MEIGETSU KA

Haruki read the English translation.

SNOW FALLEN ON SNOW

AND THIS EVENING

THE FULL MOON OF NOVEMBER

At the bookstore's exit, he more or less repeated what they had taught him: It's a present, please. Puresento—onegai shimasu. There must be something missing to unite those words. There must be a way of saying the words more eloquently, a more appropriate intonation. A gesture with his head, an inclination of his neck of which he was ignorant. The features of his face and the shape of his body were an insult to his ignorance.

But it was an understandable message. Puresento. Present. Onegai shimasu. Please.

He handed the book to the saleswoman with both hands: he had at least learned that gesture. The respect for objects. His negligent way of handling the material world, when it manifested itself, was an insult received in silence. An invisible annoyance. A shadow that should not be there, but was.

Little by little, as the days and now the weeks had gone by since he had first set his feet in Bashō's land, Haruki had begun to adjust to a consciousness of everything that surrounded him. He learned to use both hands to give and receive objects, cards, papers, purchases, whatever it might be.

Puresento—onegai shimasu, he said to the bookstore saleswoman.

She responded with a smile and multiple nods, and an additional fistful of words that Haruki did not understand.

She nimbly picked up a sheet of wrapping paper and began to fold, pleat, twist it in such a way that for Haruki it was almost hypnotic. Thin, tiny, pale hands. Without the long, multicolored, decorated nails he had seen on so many women in so many places in Japan, especially on young women. Short nails. Perhaps a requirement demanded by the job.

She seemed to be engaged in an origami demonstration. Haruki asked himself what the result would be. A star. A cricket. A samurai helmet. When the paper's number of folds and pleats proved sufficient to the girl with the thin hands, she picked up the book and placed it on the wrapping paper, off to the side. Then she continued with the folds, rapidly but apparently calm, efficiently but apparently concentrated, gently but apparently confident. Somewhat mechanically, but apparently caring.

Haruki had the impression that he would never manage to assign an adverb for that. The girl who dedicated herself completely to the wrapping paper that she was folding, and who, at the same time, appeared to be doing nothing more than her obligation. The Zen nun wrapping up a book as a gift. Efficiency completed ritualistically.

He felt like touching her to see if she was real. But he might receive a shock, if he were to do that. An electric shock. A thermal shock. He stood there watching, fascinated, as she finished. That human being so different, so unlike himself.

Alone in Tokyo. In his ryōkan in Asakusa, he had placed the bag containing the book for Celina on the table.

He no longer remembered word for word the Bashō haiku that

he had found in the book. He only knew that it spoke of snow fallen on snow.

Snow and snow. Snow plus snow. Snow in the snow. White on white. White added to white. A visual kindness. A concession.

There was no way to better compose the image of snow fallen on snow if not with those words. Yuki to yuki. Snow and snow. To say less would not be enough. To say more would be superfluous. As would be superfluous anything that Haruki might possibly think about that poem. It was enough to let it rest, to let it fall like snow fallen on snow in the imagined background of his eyes. Listen to its cottony, white silence. Snow fallen on snow in the Japanese-style room of his ryōkan in Asakusa, Tokyo.

Snow and snow, although summer had begun in the Northern Hemisphere, although it had advanced to the twenty-sixth day of June. It was now the wee hours of the morning and Haruki was not sleepy.

He had read that white was, in Japan, the color of mourning. He laced his fingers at the back of his neck and just lay there, face up.

Alice

The things that reminded her of Alice were never grandiose, they never had the luster of the main plot. On the contrary, they were small things, measured with the negligence of everyday life.

The day she pushed a bean up her nose. The yellow swimsuit that lasted two summers and how profoundly sad she was when it no longer fit her.

"Air," the poem by Vinícius de Moraes that Boca Livre sang: When I am weak my name is breeze, and if I whistle, it's quite a hoot. When I am strong, my name is wind. And when I stink, my name is toot.

The English-Portuguese junior dictionary that she had never used but of which she was very proud.

The dried leaves that she used to bring home and paste into a notebook after properly smoothing them out, not in her English-Portuguese junior dictionary, which was small, but inside one of Marco's colossal dictionaries.

The day she decided to convert to Hinduism, at the age of six, after falling passionately in love with an image of Krishna playing the flute.

The first play they took her to see. A terrible play, at the

Princesa Isabel Theater in Copacabana. *The Lion King* copied word for word from the American film, with all the music on tape. The way the play fascinated her all the same, and she simply had to ask for autographs from all the badly costumed animals at the end.

Her adoration for hens, which for years on end reigned supreme in the position of her favorite animal, outclassing the traditional ponies, bunnies, dogs, cats, the imposing lions and panthers, the eccentric iguanas and hippos. Her difficulty in remembering to begin sentences with a capital letter. Her daily insistence on going to bed after 10 o'clock at night. Her passion for tamarind drops and the doll with the Mary Quant–inspired clothes, which had belonged to her aunt and been handed down to her when, at the age of forty, her aunt had finally been able to part with that small amulet from Swinging London.

Her declared and complete predilection for rock, among all the musical styles.

Her always unruly hair. Her lavender cologne. Her watermelon shampoo. Her strawberry-flavored toothpaste. Her grape-flavored lip gloss. Her flat feet. Her potato nose.

June 27th

Haruki returns to Kyoto tomorrow. I received an answer from his publisher with Yukiko Sakade's e-mail address. I wrote to her.

25th day
SENNA RETURNS TO ŌTSU. FUMIKUNI AND JŌSŌ COME TO VISIT US.

WITH THE HUT OF FALLEN PERSIMMONS AS A THEME: BY JŌSŌ.

IN THE RECESSES OF MOUNT SAGA, IN THE COMPANY OF BIRDS
AND FISH
I LIVE IN A RUSTIC DWELLING, AS A MAN OF THE FIELDS
ON THE BRANCHES THERE ARE STILL NO EGGS OF THE
RED DRAGON
BUT IN THE GREEN FOLIAGE LIES ALL I REQUIRE TO TRACE
MY VERSES.

A VISIT TO LADY KOGŌ'S TOMB.
BY JŌSŌ.

IN ANGUISH, FILLED WITH RESENTMENT, SHE FLED THE
IMPERIAL PALACE
BENEATH THE AUTUMN MOON, IN THE WINDS THAT SWEEP THE
FIELDS.
IN THOSE YEARS LONG AGO, THE MINISTER FOUND HER THANKS
TO THE SOUND OF HER KOTO.
WHERE MIGHT BE NOW HER SOLITARY TOMB AMONGST THE
BAMBOO AND THE TREES?

BARELY GERMINATED
THEN SPROUTING PROFUSELY
PERSIMMON SEEDS

medashi yori
futaba ni shigeru
kaki no sane
(FUMIKUNI)

WRITTEN ALONG THE ROAD:

SINGS THE CUCKOO
AND IT IS ALL THE SAME: ELMS,
PLUM TREES, CHERRY TREES

hototogisu

naku ya enoki mo

ume sakura

(Jōsō)

TWO ADMIRABLE LINES BY KŌ ZANKOKU:

CHIN MUKI SEARCHED FOR INSPIRATION BEHIND
   CLOSED DOORS
SHIN SHŌYU WORKED WITH HIS PAINTBRUSH IN FRONT
   OF HIS GUESTS.

OTOKUNI COMES TO VISIT ME AND SPEAKS OF EDO. HE ALSO
BRINGS ME A BOOK OF LIGHT HAIKU, COMPOSED IN THE TIME
THAT IT TAKES A CANDLE TO BURN DOWN A HALF AN INCH. I
SELECT THE FOLLOWING:

   THE BOX OF MEDICINES
   THE MONK CARRIES
   PRESSED TO HIS HEART.

   THE USUI MOUNTAIN PASS:
   IT IS BEST TO PROCEED ON HORSEBACK

hanzoku no

kōyakuire wa

futokoro ni

Usui no tōge

umazo kashikoki

(KIKAKU)

   A BASKET AT HIS WAIST,
   HIS SPIRIT DISTURBED BY THE MOON

BESET BY AN AUTUMN WINDSTORM

HE GIVES IT TO AN EXILE

IN A COTTAGE

koshi no ajika ni
kuruwasuru tsuki

nowaki yori
runin ni watasu
koya hitotsu
(KIKAKU)

ON MOUNT UTSU:

SLEEPING IN

A WOMAN'S NIGHTCLOTHES

COMBATING LIES

ALLOWS ONE TO PURIFY THE SPIRIT

Utsu no yama
onna ni yo yogi o
karite neru

itsuwari semete
yurusu shōjin
(KIKAKU)

SINCE THE SIXTEENTH HOUR, WIND, RAIN, AND THUNDER; HAIL
FALLS. WHEN THE DRAGON CROSSES THE SKY, HAIL FOLLOWS.

THERE ARE HAILSTONES THAT WEIGH ABOUT A HALF AN OUNCE,
THE LARGER ONES ARE LIKE APRICOTS, THE SMALLER ONES ARE
LIKE SMALL CHESTNUTS.

Silence was a place within the heart. The silence perhaps covered up the indispensable forgiveness, the armistice, the silence was a permanence. Celina was thinking about silence when she got off at the same Keage subway station that she had used to go to the Philosopher's Walk. Inside the subway car a recording announced the stop in Japanese and in English.

She bought a drink from the automated vending machine. A small can of Pocari Sweat, an energy drink. She didn't like it. She drank it down all the same.

The morning was muggy and hazy. The silence echoed in Celina's ears. She went through the small tunnel in front of the subway station and continued down a narrow street, bordered by delicate, half-hidden gardens behind unimposing walls, Konchiin Street. But it offered her no shelter. Somehow her two empty hands deprived of the company of other hands insisted on weighing down heavily, like body parts made fragile, like convalescents.

And that's what they were. They were still convalescents. That's the message they sent to Celina, while her feet momentarily weren't sure of themselves. Her traveling feet, totems, the amulets that she cultivated and needed in order to hide the hard emptiness of the palms of her hands.

Let it ache, that emptiness. I don't have Alice's small hand glued to my right hand, slightly sweaty, her plastic ring that was a free gift inside a box of cereal, nor Marco's angular hand caressing my left hand, his two fingers unwittingly drawing my lifeline.

And the silence was permanent. Along Konchiin Street, bordered by low walls that only partially hid their secrets. There was something strange about all that. Was the dream unraveling? Was it almost time to wake up? Was Venus already visible in the sky, to the east, anticipating the rising of a symbolic sun?

Celina stopped before a temple. The Konchiin, part of the great Nanzenji complex. She bought a ticket. She walked over to the pond dedicated to Benten, the goddess of fortune. A particularly beautiful place in the autumn, from what she had read. But it was summer. And yet.

The aquatic plants, the bushes trimmed until perfectly rounded, the trees with branches that stretched out and thrust up as if wanting to blend in with the scenery.

Celina was alone. On that day, at that moment, there was no one else before the Benten-ike.

Tears were taking shape in her eyes. They came from afar. They rubbed against her eyelids. And they remained hidden away. Celina sat down on a bench and closed her eyes for a long time. The smell of that place. The discreet sounds of that place, measuring the silence. The summer heat, not yet very intense, on her bare arms, on her slightly sweaty legs beneath her skirt, on her face. On her neck.

The not yet intense heat on her body.

And if the world could live off nothing more than that beauty: the pond and the gardens and the Zen temple in Kyoto. And if speed were to cease, and if impulses were to hide, and if words were to desist, and if within that beauty things were to diminish, diminish, shrink, grow small, until they became a mere throbbing core devoid of dangers like hope, desire, decisions.

Would death be like that? Celina squeezed her eyes shut for an instant, then relaxed them once again. To die: Would it be a sort of acceptance? Would it be to make a pact with that small nucleus of existence and go closing the doors, the floodgates, until what remained was barely there? And then to give up on that as well? To abandon that, to immerse yourself into nothingness, into the end, into nothing at all, a snap of the fingers, click, and that assembly of bones, muscles, viscera, empty spaces, electric currents, emotions, chemical reactions, and the thoughts that were you, that pretended to unite together under a stage name (What difference does it make if you become a part of history or not?), all of that just simply evaporates? In the heat of a summer morning in Kyoto—for example?

Celina opened her eyes. They were still dry. In front of her the pond, the Benten-ike, reflecting the scenery in the places that were not yet covered by aquatic plants.

Marco and Yukiko

There was a day that Celina was washing the dishes and she broke a glass. One of those long, thin ones, with some indentations at the base.

On the kitchen counter, next to the sink, were her new sunglasses. She had bought them that afternoon, at a sunglass shop in Copacabana. The frames were slightly oval, dark brown, with beige details. The saleswoman had said: They look beautiful on you and they match that marvelous coat you're wearing. Marvelous coat? Celina felt like asking. Are you kidding? I bought it on sale at a crummy store, it didn't even cost twenty reais.

They were up there, on the counter next to the sink. Celina was washing the dishes, the other glass hit against the long, thin one and scratched a curved, upside down V, quite pretty actually, on the edge. A perfectly symmetrical crack. Celina couldn't help but admire it. Too bad there were only two. Now there was just one.

That night Marco opened a bottle of wine while Alice watched cartoons on the television in the living room and he poured a glass for himself, a glass for Celina. They made a toast standing up while she straightened up the kitchen.

Stop cleaning, he said.

She laughed. I broke a glass this afternoon.

She showed him the symmetrical scars, the double scratches on the glass.

Marco said No big deal, it's just a glass.

They ate standing up in the kitchen, crumbly toast and salty snacks with a hot salsa that he had made. A family recipe. In the living room, Alice watched cartoons on the television out of the corner of her eye while she ate noodles and the hot salsa. Alice liked spicy food.

Celina went to wash the rest of the dirty dishes. At her side, Marco was reading the label on some product. The voices of the cartoon characters could be heard in the kitchen, and some funny noises. She picked up two champagne flutes that were sitting there from the night before. On New Year's Eve, Marco had bought some champagne that had come with the two flutes as a free gift. They were pretty. Thin. Dainty. She thought about the glass she had broken earlier. She washed the flutes carefully, and placed them to dry overturned and leaning in the corner of the sink.

A careless movement, a slip of the fingers: one of the flutes fell before she could even come to the rescue. She couldn't even stretch out her arm. The champagne flute traced its path to the floor and it was not in the mood to be interrupted. An exclamation from Celina, and the shrill sound of the thin glass shattering.

Jesus, Marco said, not again. And it had to be one of those.

Celina looked down at the floor covered with shards of glass.

I'm sorry, I know you liked it.

But why on earth did you put it to dry that way? All lopsided, leaning against the dish drainer? Wouldn't it have been better to clear out the drainer first?

Yes. But I always do it that way.

Well, think about it so it won't happen again in the future. Be a little more careful.

Celina was holding some of the glass shards in her hands. She looked at Marco. She put the shards of the glass into the trashcan and went out down the hall, without saying a word, to the bathroom. There, she locked the door (she rarely locked the door) and turned on the shower.

That night, in bed, after reading to Alice, after making Alice brush her teeth and pee and put on her pajamas, Celina was lying down staring up at the ceiling. At her side, Marco was lying down, staring up at the ceiling. He fiddled with the remote control of the turned-off television. She fiddled with a bottle of moisturizing lotion. She poured out a little, rubbed it on her legs. He turned the remote control over and over between his fingers.

She looked at him. Serious, both of them. Outside the almost imperceptible sound of the rain that had just begun to fall.

It's raining, he said.

She slipped her hand into his. With the tips of his fingers he pulled back a strand of hair that had fallen over her eyes. She felt desire rising up through her stomach to her mouth that latched on to his. It was a wave. A turmoil. Her mouth lightly grazing his ear. His shoulders. The inside of his arms. To watch him shudder. Feel him shudder and touch him more lightly to make him tremble all the more. Touch him with her lips and with her tongue on his ribs, count his ribs with her breath and the tips of her teeth, touch him with her tongue in the curve of his waist, his stomach, feel the hairs that grew around his navel brush against her. Celina opened her legs and sat on him and he was hard beneath the fabric of his shorts. He ran his fingers along the seam of her panties. With both hands, he held her thighs, and pulled her higher, higher up, until that hottest spot of her body was right there, above his face. With his hand, he pushed aside her panties. With his tongue, he forced a loud moan from her.

JUNE 27TH

I can imagine the reason I've forgotten how to cry. Perhaps the water from the tears hinders the journey. Perhaps it clouds the maps. Early this morning, when I was taking my bath, I tried. I filled the bathtub, poured in some liquid soap that barely foamed, that only gave me a more or less milky surface with inconsistent bubbles. I took off my clothes and looked at myself in the mirror. I tried. I looked into my own eyes, it had been a while since I'd noticed their color. Was that ever important? I looked at my breasts, at my breasts that had appeared when I was twelve years old. At my two arms. I didn't remember to straighten my shoulders. I looked at my eyes again.

I crawled into the tub, the water only slightly tepid, today it's a bit warmer than yesterday I think. My body was hidden beneath the water and the creamy surface of the soap. My bended knees were exposed. And my feet, resting against the end of the tub.

I tried. I closed my eyes and I tried. Who knows but that immersed there, in that fraternal element, I might be able to once again produce tears, to convince my tearducts to abandon their strike, their retreat, to rebel against their malfunctioning.

Nothing. Or maybe some sign, a new weight rising up through

the bones of my face, as if I were almost managing to succeed? A
weight so discreet, so gentle that I might not even have noticed it.
But my eyes remained dry. I submerged my head into the
water, the strange silence of that element that is not and never
was mine plugged my ears. My face remained out of the water.
Dry.

26th day

BARELY GERMINATED

THEN SPROUTING PROFUSELY

PERSIMMON SEEDS

> *medashi yori*
> *futaba ni shigeru*
> *kaki no sane*
> (FUMIKUNI)

AS DUST ON THE FIELDS

DEUTZIA FLOWERS SCATTERED ABOUT

> *batake no chiri ni*
> *kakaru unohana*
> (BASHŌ)

A SNAIL

INSECURE, HESITANT

ITS TENTACLES ASWAY

> *katatsumuri*
> *tanomoshigenaki*
> *tsuno furite*
> (KYORAI)

WHILE SOMEONE DRAWS WATER FROM THE WELL
I WAIT FOR THE BUCKET

hito no kumu ma o
tsurube matsu nari
(Jōsō)

MOON AT DAYBREAK:
MIGHT THE USUAL MESSENGER
BE COMING UP THE ROAD?

ariake ni
sando bikyaku no
yuku yaran
(Ōtokuni)

27th day
NO ONE APPEARS. I SPEND THE ENTIRE DAY IN BED.

With his computer perched on a table at a Starbucks on Miyuki Street, in Ginza, Haruki was drinking a green tea Frappuccino. He had passed by the Tsukiji fish market, when it was barely dawn, to see one of the famous tuna auctions. He had read in some informative brochure on Tokyo that the transactions there could hit as much as 17 million dollars a day. There were numerous tourists. Filming, shooting photographs. This visibly irritated the traders. With or without irritations, the numbers were impressive. Two thousand five hundred dead tuna per day at the market. As Haruki well knew, Japan had been fishing more tuna than was permitted. The fish was in danger of extinction.

One day, on one of his journeys, Bashō passed by the Tsujiki fish market, having left his banana hut in Fukagawa, in the direction of the deep north.

The dead fish filled Haruki with sadness. The glazed eyes and the half-open mouths, like commas pointing downward. Mentally Haruki drew the dead fish in a watercolor. The colors were red and white.

From there, very close to the Sumida River banks, he went to visit Namiyoke Inari–jinja, the Shinto shrine for protection from the ocean waves, devoted to the divinity Inari, sometimes represented as a fox. It was old, the sanctuary. From centuries ago. From the time of Bashō. Today Namiyoke Inari was something of a guardian shrine for the fish market and its merchants.

It was barely past seven in the morning when he went into the Starbucks and ordered a green tea Frappuccino and sat down and placed his computer, which he had hauled along on his shoulder, on top of the table, and reread the message from Yukiko.

The message from Yukiko Sakade, his Bashō translator who was neither his nor Bashō's and was perhaps much too small to be seen by the human eye or much too large, like a supernova or a god.

The message from Yukiko Sakade, saying that she had exchanged e-mail with his assistant Celina. So, then, you're in Japan. In Tokyo, according to her. Searching for traces of the traveler Matsuo Bashō.

The message that Yukiko must have typed with her strong fingers making too much noise on the keyboard. What a surprise, Haruki, you in Japan.

What a surprise, Yukiko, you on my computer screen on a table at the Starbucks on Miyuki Street. What a surprise, my little spider thread.

I miss you.

Who said, who thought, who felt, who wrote that?

Your assistant told me that she went with you to help you through the bureaucratic red tape and as an interpreter.

He could not help but smile. Celina, his interpreter.

What a surprise, Haruki, you in Japan. The other day I was looking at a sketch of yours again. A sketch you did of me.

The message from Yukiko Sakade.

I miss you. I missed you before I even met you. I miss you now.

The fish at the Tsujiki market had half-open mouths, like commas pointing downward. Glazed eyes. A sadness of centuries.

Celina

In her backpack, Celina carried her diary and the diary of Bashō. Some money for food and transportation. She went by bus to her habitual station, Katsura. From there she had to catch the train to Arashiyama Station. And go by foot to her final destination.

It was strange to spend so many days without saying practically anything. Without exchanging a word with the rest of the world, other than some brief requests at counters, awkward and rapid greetings, laconic thank yous. Her voice was like a butterfly's cocoon inside her throat, executing some sort of internal transformation. Her voice seemed to carefully balance itself above that category—the bare minimum.

The bare minimum. The soft beat of a heart made of strange, foreign, hard-to-memorize words.

And that name, which was also in the heart's semantic reign: Rakushisha. A warm and slightly raspy name.

Rakushisha. A name nice to pronounce.

Rakushisha. You could feel the grains of the consonants on your tongue.

It was still morning. When she got off the train at Arashiyama Station, Celina stopped to buy an apple juice from an automated vending machine, for 120 yen. The silence was weightless. There was almost no one else there. The few people passing by seemed to take care so as not to bruise the world.

There were bicycles for rent. Celina thought about it. They cost 700 yen. She greeted the man who rented the bicycles with a nod.

Konnichi wa. Good morning. She made a gesture with her index finger that symbolized the number one. By then she knew that there were different ways of counting for different types of things in Japanese. But there was a more or less generic way of counting that helped avoid terribly embarrassing situations. Hitotsu, she said: one, underlining with her hand gesture.

Celina wasn't sure if she still knew how to ride a bicycle. The myth that it was something you never forgot was nothing more than that: a myth. Almost everything was subject to being forgotten. Countless other things insisted on not being forgotten. And thus her memory remained submissive to her heart.

She was going to Sagano, the quiet Kyoto district where Rakushisha, the cottage mentioned in Matsuo Bashō's diary, was located. She crossed Arashiyama Park on bicycle, seeing a few Japanese tourists, elderly without appearing to be so, in their cloth hats, in their plain clothes, and reached Togetsu-kyō, the Moon-crossing Bridge. Imagine yourself on the moon. With no gravity. The bicycle pedals seemed so strange beneath her feet. So strange, a metallic body, another velocity. But nonetheless, she pedaled, and pedaled, and crossed the moon that was also the Ōi River and the stones washed by the water.

She consulted her map when she reached the other side. She took what appeared to be the most obvious path and passed the tourist information booth without stopping. She didn't want information. By chance she decided to turn to the left immediately after the booth. Just by chance. There were a few charming small shops and the street was narrow and there were trustworthy-looking people turning there as well.

Suddenly the path was closed in by bamboo. She had read about a path around there that went through the bamboo. The map announced BANBOO PATH in English, with ideograms below. Perhaps bamboo was written in English with an M and not with an N. She wasn't sure.

The daylight ventured cautiously into the bamboo. Very low down, close to the base of the tallest groves, everything was full of shadows. To one side, immediately after a small marker with the inscription—may peace reign on earth—in several languages, two or three handicraft vendors. One of them greeted Celina as she passed. And then the world once again belonged to her alone and to her small, two-wheeled vehicle. Her wheels lightly crunching on the carpet of uniform bamboo shadows.

How could she possibly not think of Alice.

How could she possibly think of Alice, resign herself to reduce her to a thought.

Celina turned her face. To her left, the entrance to a temple. That was what it appeared to be. It had also leapt into her path. She turned in, went over to the ticket counter. The element of surprise had led her to Tenryūji. She bought a ticket, left her bicycle next to the entrance. Tenryūji, said the brochure: Temple of the Celestial Dragon. World Heritage Site. World heritage calmly sitting there in its solitude on an atypical day—probably on the weekends that place must be packed. But not today.

JUNE 28TH

In the Tenryūji gardens a man talks very loudly on his cell phone. Farther along, another man smells a hydrangea, an extemporaneous flower, it is summer and no one can explain why it's not raining yet. Summer begins with the rainy season, tsuyu. Hydrangeas are flowers that have no scent. In the interior of the temple it is silent. The silhouette of a boy seated on the floor, his legs crossed, his back slightly bent over, is outlined against the rectangle of light that shines into the temple.

Crows, a single lotus flower in bloom, hydrangeas. The Japanese man talking loudly on the cell telephone and the other man smelling hydrangeas.

Some uniformed students. The vegetarian lunch costs 3,000 yen and I prefer not to eat lunch. Not at that price. I have Bashō's diary with me, and we retire to a corner. I forget about cell phones and the impulse to find perfume in flowers that have no perfume.

28th day

IN A DREAM, I EVOKE TOKOKU, AND I AWAKEN IN TEARS. WHEN THE SPIRITS COMMUNICATE, WE DREAM. IF OUR YIN IS DEPLETED, WE DREAM OF FIRE. IF OUR YANG IS DRAINED, WE DREAM OF WATER. WHEN A BIRD FLIES CARRYING HAIR IN ITS BEAK, YOU DREAM THAT YOU ARE FLYING, WHEN YOU SLEEP WITH A SASH AROUND YOUR WAIST, YOU DREAM OF A SERPENT, THEY SAY. *Zhenzhong ji*, DREAMS OF THE LAND OF HUAIAN, AND ZHUANGZI'S BUTTERFLY DREAM—ALL HAVE A LOGIC TO THEM AND ARE NOT COMPLETELY OUT OF THE ORDINARY. THE

DREAMS THAT I HAVE ARE NEITHER THE DREAMS OF A WISE MAN NOR THOSE OF A GREAT MAN. DURING THE DAY I ALLOW MYSELF TO FLOW IN THE RHYTHM OF MY DAYDREAMING AND, WHEN NIGHT COMES, MY DREAMS ARE OF THE SAME NATURE. IN TRUTH, THE DREAM I HAD ABOUT HIM IS WHAT THEY CALL AN OBSESSIVE DREAM. FOR THAT MAN, WHO WAS DEEPLY DEVOTED TO ME, HAD FOLLOWED ME TO MY NATIVE VILLAGE IN IGA; AT NIGHT HE SHARED MY BED AND, TAKING UPON HIMSELF HIS SHARE OF THE WEARINESS OF MY PILGRIMAGES, FOR ONE HUNDRED DAYS HE FOLLOWED ME LIKE A SHADOW. AT TIMES HAPPY, AT TIMES SAD, HIS AFFECTION PENETRATED ME TO THE DEPTHS OF MY SOUL, AND, WITHOUT A DOUBT, I DREAMT OF THIS SO THAT I MIGHT NOT BE ABLE TO FORGET HIM. UPON AWAKENING, TEARS DRENCHED MY SLEEVES.

Upon awakening, my eyes were dry. Today is Alice's birthday. Today would have been Alice's birthday. But Alice's birthdays ended when she turned seven. When I remember Alice, when I think of Alice—but how can I reduce her to a memory, how can I reduce her to a thought?—the world is gloaming.

In the research center's apartment, in Kyoto, I have a pair of zori for Alice. How can I reduce them to the absurdity that they are, how not to have bought them, how not to have seen Alice's feet in the feet of the Japanese girl who was petting a white cat, in the corner of the shop?

Upon awakening, my eyes were dry.

Today is Alice's thirteenth birthday, but the sandals were for the seven-year-old Alice, they were for Alice as she was crystallized into all we could ever know about her. Today is not Alice's thirteenth birthday.

The bicycle I rented rests immobile at the temple entrance. Alice's bicycle was given away. As were her clothes, her toys, her books, her CDs from the Disquinho Collection, which I also had in vinyl, when I was a child, decades earlier. *Peter and the Wolf.* The Brazilian tale, *The Party in the Sky. The Tin Soldier,* which would make me so sad.

Seven-year-old Alice wearing her zori is an image I try to imprint on my retinas. Who knows, perhaps this would create the inverse path and she could move from that improbability to another improbability, that of stretching out her small, thick-soled feet toward me (she was always working on thickening those feet) so I could put the Japanese sandals on her.

Look, Alice, how pretty they are on you.

But I can't ride a bicycle in them.

That's true, you can't. They're for other occasions.

They're pretty. Do all Japanese girls wear sandals like that?

No. Just some of them.

For one hundred days she followed me like a shadow, and afterward for another one hundred times one hundred days, until I lost count and the world began to be measured in steps, one after another, to keep from disintegrating. The planet would solidify as I stepped on it. The hot lava would turn into crust, would turn into earth. For one hundred times one hundred days she followed me like a shadow and for one hundred times one hundred days I stretched out my hands behind my back to try and reach her. Touch her. Press her small body to mine and hear her voice complaining you're hugging me too tight, Mom.

Upon awakening, my eyes were dry and I only felt the urgency to obey my movements like a Labrador in a yellow raincoat that follows his owner.

It is not raining in Arashiyama. Bicycles go by and a rice field lines up its greenness beneath the sun. A few people. She is looking for the sign with three ideograms: 落柿舍. Rakushisha. The Hut of Fallen Persimmons, which hosted the poet Matsuo Bashō more than three hundred years earlier.

On the way, Celina passed through Torokko Saga Station, where the Sagano Romantic Train departs. Some couples were waiting for the next departure. Celina bought a green tea ice cream.

Her camera batteries are dead. She decides to trust in the miniscule handicraft store next door. She enters: Sumimasen! No one answers. It takes a few seconds for a woman with short steps and a secret smile to come from within. Her hair is pulled back in a bun. Celina shows her the two batteries. The woman picks up a package and says the price.

What country are you from, she asks, in English.

Brazil.

Oh, Brazil! Carnival! Soccer!

She pulls out a guestbook. Could you write something here? In your language, please. I don't have any messages written by someone from Brazil yet.

The secret smile. Celina takes the book and sees messages from people from so many different places. Canada. Portugal. France. Some people pasted in their cards. With a shaky hand, she writes a few lines.

When she finishes, the owner of the handicraft shop goes into the back and returns with a small roll of paper. She unrolls it: it is calligraphy scroll that she has made. A love poem. She rerolls it. She offers it to Celina with both hands and a bow.

The calligraphy scroll in one hand, the camera with the new batteries in the other, Celina leaves the small handicraft store. In front of her lies a rice field. She walks a few yards and finds the sign she has been looking for, with the ideograms she has learned to recognize: Rakushisha. Three ideograms drawn with black ink on a wooden board, hanging on a vine-covered wall.

The calligraphy scroll in one hand, the camera in the other. Water blurs Celina's eyes as she walks her bicycle toward Rakushisha, the cottage that belonged to Kyorai and where his master Bashō stayed for the last time in the fifth lunar month of the fourth year of Genroku.

On the horizon, the silhouetted mountains. The water in Celina's eyes, which streams forth from a newly discovered source, which streams down for the saleswoman from the handicraft store in Sagano and for Alice's birthday and for Celina, who cannot squeeze shadows in her arms, and for Marco, and for the dead on the fields of battle, and for Haruki, who is returning from Tokyo at this very moment, and for Yukiko, the woman that Haruki loves, the woman that loves Haruki. Down her face streams salty water from her own internal rainy season, her own intimate tsuyu, which now begins.

To travel is for the journey in itself. It is to have the road beneath your feet. In front of Rakushisha, the rice field lines up its greenness beneath the sun.

Haruki

The scenery already looks familiar. The return train to Kyoto,
the bullet train that departed from Tokyo. Haruki already is almost
one of them, he almost belongs there. Retracing your route means
taking note of yourself in the world. Leaving a footprint, planting a
flag. Retracing your route etches a scar into the scenery. It is not
just the lack of commitment of the one-way path.

    I miss you. I missed you before I met you. I miss you now.
That means retracing a route. Returning to you and to how I have
missed you and will always miss you. Even if I am at your side.
Even if I feel your hand in mine and your body producing waves
of heat. The discreet sweat of your hand in mine.

    Is there another way? If it is essential (and it is essential) to
have you, is there another way?

AND IF there is no other way?

    AND IF the passage that we make through one another's lives
is this? Only this? The passage of a traveler?

    AND IF I continue sketching you obsessively as I did for a
year, for the next ten or twenty or thirty years?

    AND IF our encounters come without the label of family, of

city hall, of wedding bands, of dinnertime, of the newspaper at the doorstep in the morning, of grocery shopping, of slippers by the bed, of toilet seats, of toothbrushes, of libraries and of night-clubs, of messages stuck on the refrigerator door, of coffee cups on the counter with black circles in the bottom, of the same bath towels, of the same places at the table, of the favorite brand of shampoo, of the answering machine, of the adjustments of the toaster and the car's rearview mirrors, of the bills at the end of the month, of friends in common?

AND IF it is crucial to recognize our own fragility in the fragility of what we are together? Travelers?

AND IF I crush with the tips of my fingers this ridiculous gesture of yours to carry your husband's last name together with your own last name?

AND IF I remove from all the dictionaries of all the languages these categories, these universal absolutes?

JUNE 28TH *(At Rakushisha)*

Persimmons are the eggs of red dragons.

The Hut of Fallen Persimmons belonged to the poet Kyorai, and it was there that his master Bashō stayed for the last time in the fifth lunar month of the fourth year of Genroku.

On the horizon, the silhouetted mountains. In the garden, a gorintō, a monument of five stones piled on one another repre-senting earth, water, fire, wind, and air, honors all of the haiku poets of the past, present, and future. Mosquitoes flutter about. The sky clouds up ever so gently.

Let Bashō's land arrive through my five senses, let it nestle in my lungs, imprint itself onto my fingertips, undulate in green tea on my tongue, let a great Zen temple bell resonate in my ears, even if mixed in with the profuse and distinct timbres of cell phones.

Above all, let Bashō's land engrave itself onto my eyes and onto the memory of my eyes, even though it be amidst all the visual pollution of this Japan three hundred years later.

See the frog leap in the old pond, listen to the faint murmur of the water, and then observe the concentric circles spread out and disappear.

29th day

I READ THE POEM ABOUT TAKADACHI IN ŌSHŪ, IN THE *Ichinin isshu* ANTHOLOGY.

Last day of the month

TAKADACHI RISES UP AS HIGH AS THE SKY AND THE STARS

THE KOROMO RIVER FLOWS INTO THE SEA

THE MOON IS LIKE AN ARCHER'S BOW

SUCH DESCRIPTIONS OF LANDSCAPES DO NOT CORRESPOND TO REALITY.

UNLESS ONE ACTUALLY GOES TO THE PLACE,

EVEN THE ANCIENT ONES CANNOT CREATE AUTHENTIC POEMS.

On the train back to Kyoto, the landscape whips by before Haruki's eyes. But it is just an impression. Time has stopped indefinitely.

At the Hut of Fallen Persimmons, Celina walks among the small stone monuments, in the garden. As she walks, time has stopped indefinitely.

KYORAI'S MASTER, BASHŌ, VISITED RAKUSHISHA THREE TIMES: IN 1689, 1691, AND 1694. WHEN HE VISITED THE SECOND TIME,

HE STAYED FROM THE EIGHTEENTH DAY OF THE FOURTH LUNAR
MONTH UNTIL THE FIFTH DAY OF THE FIFTH. THE DIARY HE
WROTE ON THAT OCCASION IS CALLED *Saga nikki* AND IT WAS
PUBLISHED IN THE THIRD YEAR OF HŌREKI (1753). HIS LAST
VISIT TO RAKUSHISHA WAS APPROXIMATELY FOUR MONTHS
BEFORE HIS DEATH.

One day Celina was walking to the subway station, having just left
DETRAN on Presidente Vargas Avenue. Then her cell phone
rang, inside her purse, and it was a ring capable of knocking the
earth off of its axis for a second.

It was the same ring as always. A simple, telephone-like ring.
None of those emulations of Mozart symphonies. And, nevertheless, it was not the same, it would never again be the same.

Was it irony, some sort of joke played by that false god of the
apocalypse that she was leaving the National Department of
Transportation? The car: a total loss. Marco: two broken ribs and
an open fracture of the foot. And Alice. Alice, an open fracture of
the heart, of the memory, within the embrace that could no longer
enfold anything, not even shadows, not even ghosts.

So it was that she broke all the links, all the ties, everything
that led to him. Except for the heartache. For whether or not it
was his fault, he was at the wheel, whether he was distracted by
something or dozed off or made a bad maneuver—it didn't matter.
All the roads were closed down. They became overgrown by
plants. The asphalt, for lack of use, cracked open.

But the ring of that cell phone, a simple, telephone-like ring,
reverberated for all time.

It continues to reverberate here, among the stone monuments
in the Rakushisha garden. This is a fact.

What would you do, Celina had asked Marco years ago, on the night before the accident, if it were your last day with me?

He raised his eyes to her and smiled. What a thought.

It's that I'm reading this book here—she explained. A last day, and they both know it, because she's leaving, and there's nothing he can do about it.

He could go with her.

No, not in this case he can't.

Are you thinking about leaving?

She smiled, tossed her head, and lowered her eyes back to her book.

She makes her way over to the small window of the ticket booth where there are a few articles for sale. She regards the objects, one by one. She chooses a small calligraphy scroll that reproduces the last poem written by Bashō at Rakushisha.

Because she is leaving, and there is nothing he can do about it.

Onto the envelope that the Rakushisha ticket seller hands her, she writes Marco's name. She tears a leaf out of her notebook that she is using as a diary and writes: Forgive me. Together with the delicate leaf of Japanese paper she wraps the last poem written by Bashō at Rakushisha.

Haruki sees the gentle rain that begins to fall as his train approaches the Kyoto station.

Celina feels the gentle rain that begins to fall as she leafs through her diary, as she carefully places it, as well as the envelope containing the calligraphy into her backpack. As she leaves Rakushisha and gets her bicycle and looks at the rice field and the mountains silhouetted against the horizon.

This is the truth to be found in traveling. I hadn't realized.

Traveling teaches us a few things. That life is a path and not a fixed point in space. That we are like the passage of the days and the months and the years, as the Japanese poet Matsuo Bashō wrote in a travel diary, and that the one thing we do indeed possess, our only asset, is our capacity of locomotion. It is our talent for traveling.

Bashō

1st day (of the 5th lunar month)

RIYŪ, FROM THE MEISHŌ TEMPLE IN HIRATA, IN THE
PROVINCE OF ŌSHŌ, COMES TO VISIT ME.
LETTERS FROM SHŌHAKU AND FROM SENNA.

BAMBOO SHOOTS—
THOSE LEFT OVER
COVERED WITH DEW

*take no ko ya
kuinokosareshi
ato no tsuyu*
(RIYŪ)

ON THESE DAYS
CLOTHING CLINGS TO THE BODY:
IT IS NOW THE FIFTH MONTH

*kono goro no
hadagi mi ni tsuku
uzuki kana*
(SHŌHAKU)

AND UPON DEPARTING:
ANXIOUSLY AWAITED
THE FIFTH MONTH
AND THE GROOM'S RICE CAKE

mataretsuru
satsuki mo chikashi
mukochimaki
(SHŌHAKU)

2nd day

SORA COMES TO SEE ME: HE WENT TO SEE THE FLOWERS IN YOSHINO, AND TO MAKE A PILGRIMAGE TO KUMANO, THIS IS WHAT HE TELLS ME. WE TALK OF OLD FRIENDS AND OF MY DISCIPLES IN EDO.

TRAIL TO KUMANO
PUSHING THROUGH THE THICKET
SUMMER SEA

Kumanoji ya
waketsutsuireba
natsu no umi
(SORA)

MOUNT ŌMINE —
INTO THE INTERIOR OF YOSHINO
THE LAST BLOSSOMS

Ōmine ya
Yoshino no oku o
hana no hate
(SORA)

TRASH ROOM ETIQUETTE

Please be reminded of the following rules and etiquette regarding trash and the trash rooms:

- Trash Room Hours are 8:00 am to 10:00 pm;
- Please be considerate of your neighbors
- Trash must be placed in bags that are completely closed before being placed in the Trash Chute
- If the trash bag seems heavy to you, it's most likely too heavy to be placed in the Trash Chute
- Do not force trash bags into the Trash Chute; Nothing larger than a tall kitchen garbage bag
- Please call the Front Desk to arrange for pick-up of oversized items such as cardboard boxes
- Pick-ups are made from Units: Don't leave items on Trash Room floors or in the hallway
- The City prohibits construction waste, hazardous materials, and e-waste to be placed into our bins
- Bags containing cat litter or other animal waste and/or glass should be double-bagged to mitigate a mess in the Main Trash Rooms in the Garage
- Our trash company recycles at their facility so there is no alternative location for recyclables

GARAGE REMINDER

THE GARAGE CAN BE A DANGEROUS PLACE SO
PLEASE REMEMBER TO FOLLOW THE RULES FOR
YOUR SAFETY AND THE SAFETY OF OTHERS.

ALWAYS FOLLOW THE **5 MPH**
POSTED SPEED LIMIT.

ALWAYS BE ACTIVELY ON THE
LOOKOUT FOR PEDESTRIANS
AND OTHER VEHICLES.

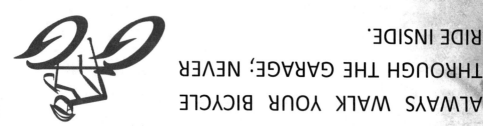

ALWAYS WALK YOUR BICYCLE
THROUGH THE GARAGE; NEVER
RIDE INSIDE.

ALSO, TO PREVENT UNAUTHORIZED ACCESS,
PLEASE ALWAYS ENSURE THAT DOORS TO THE
LOBBIES ARE CLOSED AND THAT YOU REPORT
ANY OPEN DOORS OR GATES.

WHEN THE SUN SETS, FROM THE ŌI RIVER WE GO BY BOAT UP THE TONASE RIVER, ROWING ALONG MOUNT ARASHI. THE RAIN BEGINS TO FALL AND WE RETURN AT TWILIGHT.

3rd day

LAST NIGHT'S RAIN CONTINUES TO FALL, DURING THE ENTIRE DAY AND DURING THE ENTIRE NIGHT WITHOUT STOPPING. WE CONTINUE OUR CONVERSATION OF THE THINGS AND OF THE PEOPLE OF EDO, UNTIL NIGHT TURNS TO DAWN.

4th day

EXHAUSTED BY A NIGHT OF INSOMNIA, I REMAIN LYING DOWN THE ENTIRE DAY. AFTER MIDDAY, THE RAIN CEASES. LAMENTING THAT TOMORROW I MUST LEAVE THE HUT OF FALLEN PERSIMMONS, I VISIT IT, ROOM BY ROOM.

SUMMER RAIN

PAPERS TORN OFF

MARKS ON THE WALLS

samidare ya
shikishi hegitaru
kabe no ato

落柿舎

Author's Note about the Translations

For the translation of *Saga nikki* into Portuguese, I used the Japanese editions *Bashō bunshū*, Nihon Koten Bungaku Taikei 46 (Tokyo: Iwanami Shoten, 1959) and *Bashō bunshū*, Nihon Koten Zensho 89 (Tokyo: Asahi Shinbunsha, 1962, 3rd printing). The translations of René Sieffert (in *Journaux de voyage* [Paris: Publications Orientalistes de France, 2000]) and of David Landis Barnhill (in *Bashō's Journey* [Albany: State University of New York Press, 2005]) were consulted for clarification. Comprehension of the Japanese original would not have been possible without the assistance of Sonia Ninomiya. Sarah Green translated the Bashō texts into English from my Portuguese version, also consulting the Sieffert and Barnhill works. Her translation was reviewed by Dawn Ollila.

Acknowledgments

I would like to thank those who first read these pages and those who helped make possible my visit to the land of Bashō. Most especially Gustavo Bernardo, Denilson Lopes, Ítalo Moriconi, Raquel Abi-Sâmara, Wilberth Claython Salgueiro, Arnaldo and Gilda Fábregas, Flávio Carneiro, José Luis Jobim, Ondjaki, Paulo Franchetti, Paulo Rocco, and Satomi Kitahara. I would also like to thank Denize Barros, for her memories. The Consul General of Japan at Rio de Janeiro, Kiyoshi Ishii. Ayumi Hashimoto (Tokyo), and Takao Hirota and Chie Yamamoto (Kyoto) at the Japan Foundation, Shoichi Inoue, Yukiko Okuno, and Ayako Sasaki at Nichibunken, in Kyoto. And lastly, Paulo Gurevitz.

I would also like to express my deepest appreciation to the Japan Foundation for the research fellowship awarded me.